Dearest Reader,

Camfield Novels of Love mark a very exciting era of my books with Jove. They have already published nearly two hundred of my titles since they became my first publisher in America, and now all my original paperback romances in the future will be published exclusively by them.

As you already know, Camfield Place in Hertfordshire is my home, which originally existed in 1275, but was rebuilt in 1867 by the grandfather of Beatrix Potter.

It was here in this lovely house, with the best view in the county, that she wrote *The Tale of Peter Rabbit*. Mr. McGregor's garden is exactly as she described it. The door in the wall that the fat little rabbit could not squeeze underneath and the goldfish pool where the white cat sat twitching its tail are still there.

I had Camfield Place blessed when I came here in 1950 and was so happy with my husband until he died, and _____ _____ children and grandchildren, that I know _____ and we have all b____

It is eas_____ you will enjoy the _____ lots are definitely y_____ c. They come to you, like ___ ___ _____

Bless you,

Barbara Cartland

CAMFIELD NOVELS OF LOVE
by Barbara Cartland

Other books by Barbara Cartland

A NEW CAMFIELD NOVEL OF LOVE BY

BARBARA CARTLAND

A Dream in Spain

A JOVE BOOK

A DREAM IN SPAIN

A Jove Book/published by arrangement with
the author

PRINTING HISTORY
Jove edition/September 1986

ISBN: 0-515-08673-8

Jove Books are published by The Berkley Publishing Group,
200 Madison Avenue, New York, N.Y. 10016. The words
"A JOVE BOOK" and the "J" with sunburst are trademarks
belonging to Jove Publications, Inc.

PRINTED IN THE UNITED STATES OF AMERICA

Author's Note

WHEN I visited Madrid at Easter last year I had not been to Spain for thirty years.

The history of Madrid began with the Arabs in 852, but it did not become the capital of the country until 1561, when Philip II was King.

Now, with its broad areas and ultra-modern buildings, it is one of the most densely populated and dynamic capitals in Europe. I was entranced by the exquisite architecture of the Plaza Mayor built in 1617, and the Royal Palace was more impressive than I remember and is exactly how a King's Palace should be.

I visited for the second time the grim, frightening Escorial, thirty-seven miles outside Madrid, and although filled with sightseers and bathed in sunshine, there was something eerie and menacing about the great stone building.

I have tried to encapsulate in the novel some of the emotions moving around in me. The plot sprang into my mind as from my bedroom window at the Ritz I saw the long queues forming outside the Prado even before it opened.

chapter one

1883

VALEDA, riding home through the woods, thought how lucky she was to have such an excellent horse to ride.

Her father had bought Skylark for her just before he died, and had paid more than he had intended for him.

Valeda was well aware that if she had been left with only the other horses in the stable, which were all growing old, she would have found the rides she took every morning, and if possible every afternoon, very dreary and unexciting.

Skylark, however, was always ready to give his rider what Sir Rodrick Alcester had called "a good run for his money."

As if to keep Valeda on her mettle, he shied at the bough of a tree that had fallen across the mossy path, and when she corrected him, bucked to show his independence.

Almost as if he were talking to her and telling her it

was only fun, Valeda bent forward to pat his neck.

As she rode on she had a glimpse of the Manor House in which she had been born and thought it had a beauty which exceeded that of many larger and more impressive houses in the neighbourhood.

It was, however, although she did not think of it like that, a rather dull part of the County for a young girl to live in, since there was nothing there to attract the smart society who lived half their lives in London.

Because of this, the houses were inhabited by elderly couples whose children had long grown up, married, and moved away, or else, as Sir Rodrick Alcester had been, aged widowers who had no wish to marry again.

Valeda had sometimes thought it was selfish of her to be glad that her father had not put another woman in her mother's place.

Instead, he had been quite content to run his small estate with his daughter's help and to find plenty to do, as Hermione once said spitefully, "just maundering about."

"What do you expect Papa to do?" Valeda had asked.

"Well, for one thing, he might take over the Hunt and offer better sport. That might attract a few more interesting men for us to meet out hunting instead of red-faced farmers and their hobbledehoy sons!"

Valeda had laughed, but she had understood that being so beautiful, her sister resented having no one to pay her compliments.

It was therefore, although she would have been ashamed to confess it, quite a relief when, while Hermione was staying in London with an elderly cousin, she had met the Earl of Eltsley and married him.

It had all happened so quickly that Valeda, who had

been only twelve at the time, could hardly believe it possible that one day her sister was there and they were a family, and the next she had disappeared.

After Hermione was married, months would go by without their hearing from her.

It was then, although Valeda never spoke of it, that after her father was widowed. He so seldom mentioned his elder daughter, that it seemed as if he had forgotten she ever existed.

As she grew older, Valeda became aware she was filling the place in her father's life which should have been taken by the son he never had.

He would talk to her as if she were a boy, and they planned together what should be done on the estate.

They shot pigeons in the woods and, when they were lucky, partridges in the fields, and more important than anything else, enjoyed riding every moment of the day.

Sir Rodrick had always been a very good judge of horses, and it amused him to buy cheap some animal which he sensed would prove, when it was fully trained, very much better and more valuable than it had appeared at a first glance.

Valeda found this fascinating, and through her experience of handling a wide variety of mounts she became an exceptionally fine horsewoman, although neither she nor her father thought of it as being anything unusual.

Then last winter, after Sir Rodrick had caught a chill which turned to pneumonia, and he died, Valeda found it hard to believe she was completely and utterly alone.

At first her sorrow at losing her father enveloped her like a dark cloud. Then, with the elasticity of youth, she knew she must go on living and enjoying life in the same way she had done when he was alive.

She found it, in fact, impossible to think of her father as dead, and she would find herself at the end of the day asking him if she had done the right thing, and if he was pleased at the decisions she had made.

She was sure she still heard him talking things over with her and advising her in exactly the same way as he had done over the last few years.

Now as she rode home she was saying, as if he were riding beside her:

"It is a lovely house, Papa, and all the generations of Alcesters who lived here before us have filled it with love."

She could hear her father reply:

"That is what I have had, my dear, with your mother and with you, and I have always thought myself a very lucky man."

"And I have been lucky to have such a marvellous father," Valeda would say, "and one who is so intelligent."

She had always found it fascinating to talk to her father in the evenings after dinner, when they would discuss subjects which covered all aspects of the world.

In his youth Sir Rodrick had been an ardent traveller, and he would tell Valeda stories of the countries he had visited, which to her were more fascinating than anything she could read in history books.

Because he had the gift of expressing himself both fluently and picturesquely, she often felt that she had actually travelled in Greece, France, Italy, Spain, and the North of Africa.

Local friends had at first been surprised when after Sir Rodrick died, Valeda had remained at the Manor alone.

"Surely, dear," the Lord Lieutenant's wife had said gently, "you have some relative who could come to live with you? After all, you really should have a chaperone."

Valeda had laughed.

"I assure you," she replied, "I am more than adequately chaperoned by the servants who have been with us for so long that they are far closer to me than any relative could ever be."

The Lord Lieutenant's wife pursed her lips, and Valeda went on:

"Nanny, who came to look after Hermione when she was born, has now been with us for twenty-six years, and old Banks and his wife were with Papa before he married. I think their years of service amount to thirty-three."

She had laughed again before she went on:

"They cosset me, protect me, and worry over me like so many old hens with one chick! So I promise you, I have no need of any other chaperone."

Another friend, who had loved Lady Alcester, had pleaded with Valeda to go to London.

"Now you are out of mourning it is time you made your curtsy at a 'Drawing-Room,' my dear," she said. "You should have a Season as a Débutante, attending Balls and Receptions, which were such successes where your sister was concerned."

Valeda, however, had shied away from the idea as violently as a nervous horse.

"I am quite happy here, thank you," she said firmly, "and I have no wish to go to London."

"But surely your sister realises, now that you have lost your dear father, that she should look after you?"

This was a question that was to be repeated a great number of times, and Valeda learnt to evade an argument by never answering it directly.

She knew only too well that Hermione did not want her and had no wish to trouble herself with a younger sister now that she was orphaned any more than she had shown any interest in Valeda from the time she had married.

When her father died, Hermione had sent a very large and expensive wreath and a letter to say that unfortunately she was too indisposed to attend the funeral.

Valeda was not deceived by her words of condolence, knowing that for the past seven years Hermione had never concerned herself with what was left of her family.

The only information they had about her came from the Social Columns of the newspapers, which always described her in glowing terms.

Valeda had read:

The beautiful Countess of Eltsley was wearing a gown of sky-blue velvet trimmed with satin ribbons and lace . . .

and:

There was no one more beautiful in the Ballroom than the Countess of Eltsley, whose magnificent diamond tiara eclipsed those worn by every lady present, with the exception of the Princess of Wales . . .

Sometimes there would be a photograph in a Ladies'

Magazine in which Hermione looked rather stiff, and yet, at the same time, very beautiful.

In one picture she had looked a little sad, but Valeda was sure that was due only to the incompetence of the photographer. For what could Hermione find to make her sad when she was acclaimed as a great beauty, and it was obvious that she had a husband who, because he loved her, decked her out in priceless jewels?

Then a little over a year ago Valeda had learned with consternation that quite unexpectedly the Earl of Eltsley had suffered a heart-attack and died.

Valeda had then assumed that her sister would come home.

Who else would she turn to for consolation and comfort in her loss but her family?

But although her father wrote and offered if she needed him to come to London immediately, there was no reply for nearly two weeks.

Then, at last, when they were wondering what could possibly have happened, Hermione wrote a stiff little letter to say that there was no need for anybody to worry about her, she was perfectly well and was going abroad to stay with friends in France, taking her daughter, Mirabelle, with her.

Sir Rodrick had said nothing, but Valeda, who knew him so well, was aware how hurt he had always been that Hermione had never brought his only grandchild home and he had never been invited to London to see the little girl.

Mirabelle had been sent presents at Christmas and on her birthday first by Lady Alcester when she was alive, and after she was dead by Valeda.

Sometimes Hermione wrote to thank them for the

gifts, but more often there was just a letter from the Earl's secretary acknowledging their arrival.

'I wonder who Mirabelle resembles?' Valeda often thought.

Then she knew that if Mirabelle should grow up to be as beautiful as her mother, Hermione would be jealous.

She faced the uncomfortable fact that the reason why Hermione had no wish to communicate with her or ask her to stay after her marriage was that she wanted everything for herself and had no wish to share it with anybody.

It seemed extraordinary that she should feel like this about her own sister, and yet Valeda could remember when she was quite small hearing Hermione raging at her mother and saying:

"I cannot think why you wanted to give me a sister! To have a brother would have been a little better, but actually I want to be the only child that you and Papa had and not have to share my things with anyone!"

Lady Alcester had spoken gently but firmly to her elder daughter, telling her how selfish she was being, and that she would, in fact, find it very lonely to be an only child.

Hermione had listened, but with a withdrawn expression on her face, which told Valeda that she did not believe anything her mother had said and had been speaking no less than the truth when she had asserted that she wanted to be an only child and thus to avoid all competition in the family.

"I may as well face the truth," Valeda said after her father's funeral when there was only a large wreath to represent Hermione, "I shall never see my sister again."

She felt not exactly hurt by Hermione's indifference.

It was more a sense of being deprived of something precious, something which she knew other families whose members were close to one another enjoyed and which could never be hers.

But she had grown used to being on her own, apart from a number of elderly neighbours who welcomed her whenever she called on them.

She was content with the horses and, of course, books which filled the Library, and which her father and she had enjoyed together.

Now, riding home in the sunshine, she felt as if the green corn sprouting in the fields, the mauve cuckoo-flowers in the grass, and the buttercups golden as the sun spoke to her.

They were part of her life, part of her consciousness, and she often thought they were part of every breath she drew.

She thought sometimes, when the first buds of spring could be seen in the shrubs and the hedgerows, that she could feel the very earth coming live after the winter and that it awakened something very exciting within herself.

She could feel herself growing as the buds were growing into the lush beauty of summer.

She felt that everything in Nature was not only part of herself, but could speak to her and make her feel that she, as they were, was being resurrected after the barrenness of winter.

Now, because Skylark realised he was going back to his comfortable stable, he quickened his pace to gallop across the paddock, and slowed down only as they approached the cobble-stones of the stableyard.

As they rode in, an old groom who also had been at

the Manor for a great many years came out from a stall to take hold of Skylark's bridle.

"'Ad a noice roide, Miss Valeda?" he asked.

"Lovely, thank you, Abbey," Valeda replied, "and Skylark went like the wind when he galloped over the straight meadow."

"'E can move when 'e wants."

He started to lead Skylark off towards his stable and only as he reached the door did he turn his head to say:

"There's be some'un up at t'house to see ye, Miss Valeda. A carriage arrived a short toim ago."

"I wonder who that can be?" Valeda remarked, but if old Abbey knew the answer, he did not tell her, but disappeared inside the stall.

She walked over the cobbles towards the ancient archway which led to the front of the house.

When she reached it, she could see a smart travelling carriage drawn by four well-bred horses, and sitting on the box a coachman in a distinctive livery with a cock-aded top-hat.

There was a footman wearing the same livery standing by the carriage-door, and as Valeda hurried forward, she wondered frantically who could be calling on her.

No one she could think of at the moment could have arrived in such a smart turnout, and as she hurried up the steps to the front-door, the two servants saluted her and she wondered if she should ask them who their master, or mistress, might be.

Then she decided it would be a mistake to do anything of the sort, and she walked in through the open front-door a little apprehensively, aware that her hair beneath her riding-hat was slightly untidy from the speed at which she had galloped on Skylark.

Because she had not expected to see anyone that afternoon, she was wearing an old riding-habit that was not only a little threadbare, but was actually too tight for her across the breast.

There was, however, nothing she could do about it without keeping her caller, whoever it might be, waiting for even longer.

She therefore pushed some of the curls that were rioting around her cheeks back into place and crossed the hall to open the Drawing-Room door.

This was a long, very attractive room with windows looking onto the rose-garden on the other side of it.

As she entered, Valeda had eyes only for the woman who was standing in front of the mirror over the fireplace and apparently regarding her own reflection.

For a moment all she could see was an extremely elegant silk gown of blue satin and a hat ornamented with ostrich feathers of the same colour.

Then as she shut the door behind her the woman turned and Valeda gave a gasp of astonishment.

"Hermione! Is it really you?"

Valeda thought her voice seemed to ring out almost too loudly, and there was a pause before her sister replied:

"Hello, Valeda! I might have guessed you would be out riding."

"Why did you not tell me you were coming?" Valeda asked. "And why are you here?"

"I have a very good reason for wanting to see you," Hermione answered, "and I must say, you have changed very little since we last met."

"Which was a very long time ago!"

"Yes, I know, I know," Hermione said quickly, "but

do not let us start by having recriminations over my neglect, or whatever you like to call it."

There was a little pause. Then Valeda said:

"I think Papa would have liked to see you before he died, but his death was very sudden and unexpected."

"How could I guess that was going to happen?" Hermione asked. "But it is no use raking over the past or regretting what cannot be undone. Sit down, Valeda, I want to talk to you."

"Yes, of course," Valeda agreed, "but first, would you like some tea or refreshment of some sort?"

"I have ordered it already," Hermione replied. "That old man has been here for years—what is his name?"

"Banks."

"Yes, of course. Banks said he would bring me some tea, and I am quite prepared to believe I shall have to wait until Christmas before it arrives!"

Valeda laughed.

"It will not be as bad as that, but he is growing very old."

"That is what the house looks and everything in it!" Hermione said disparagingly.

Valeda was just about to retort that as far as she was concerned, everything was perfect, then decided it would be a mistake.

Instead, she took off her riding-hat, attempted to smooth down her riotous curls, and sat down on the sofa.

Looking at Hermione standing in front of her, she thought it would be impossible for anybody to be more beautiful, or, in fact, more like a fashion-plate which had stepped straight out of an expensive magazine.

It was not only Hermione's gown that was so different from anything she had seen before, but so were the whiteness of her skin, the jewels flashing in her ears and on her long, thin fingers, and the large row of perfect pearls that encircled her lovely neck.

Because she was used to expressing her thoughts, Valeda exclaimed with an unmistakable sincerity:

"How beautiful you look, Hermione! Everything about you is absolutely perfect!"

"That is what I always intend," Hermione replied complacently.

"I see you are out of mourning," Valeda went on. "I was so very sorry to hear of your husband's death."

"It was certainly entirely unexpected," Hermione replied, "but, as you say, I am out of mourning, and there is no point in talking about the past. In fact, Valeda, it is the future I want to discuss with you now."

"The . . . future?"

It flashed through Valeda's mind, though it seemed impossible, that perhaps Hermione wished to come home.

She knew with a feeling of horror that nothing she found at the Manor would be good enough for her, and in consequence she would spoil the happiness that Valeda had always known there.

Hermione sat down in an armchair opposite the sofa on which her sister was sitting, and arranged the folds of her skirt. Then as Valeda waited she began:

"I have come home because I need your help, and I feel sure you will not refuse to give it to me."

"N-no . . . of course not," Valeda said, "but I do not see how I can help you."

"That is what I intend to tell you, if you will listen!"

There was a note in Hermione's voice which Valeda

13

well remembered was always there if she did not get exactly what she wanted and without having to wait for it.

She was curious, but at the same time very apprehensive.

"I am, as you know, a widow," Hermione began, but she did not sound as if that was something that upset her very much.

"It must be . . . difficult for you," Valeda murmured.

As if she had not spoken, Hermione continued:

"I have of course decided that I will marry again, if it is to my advantage to do so."

"Marry again!" Valeda exclaimed, realising she had been very stupid not to imagine this was a possibility.

"Stop repeating everything I say!" Hermione said sharply.

Valeda lapsed into silence, her eyes looking very large fixed on her sister's beautiful face.

"As of course you must realise, my position in the Social World is one of great importance," Hermione said complacently. "At the same time, not so important as if my husband had given me a son."

There was a note in her voice as if she blamed the Earl for the fact that she had a daughter instead. Then as if Valeda had asked the question, Hermione continued:

"There is, of course, a new Earl of Eltsley, a nephew of my late husband's for whom I have no liking, and I should therefore be quite pleased to change my name if the gentleman I have in mind asks me to be his wife."

"It seems to me impossible that anyone would not wish to marry you, Hermione."

"That is what I think myself," Hermione said, smiling, "and I am sure it is only a question of time. Now I

14

am going to be honest with you, Valeda, and tell you I was recently almost in despair of bringing him to the point."

Her voice rose as she went on:

"But now he has asked me to visit his family in Spain, and I feel certain there can be only one reason for that!"

"In Spain!" Valeda exclaimed. "Are you saying he is a foreigner?"

"He is a Spaniard," Hermione replied, "and an extremely important one. The Marquis de Silvala has a position that is second only to that of the Royal Family."

Valeda clasped her hands together.

"Oh, Hermione, how wonderful for you! And do you love him very much?"

"The question is whether he loves me enough to marry outside the very strict Court Circles that make the Spaniards more proud of themselves than any people on earth."

Valeda thought it all sounded rather frightening, but she said a little nervously, in case her sister should be annoyed:

"But, surely . . . nothing matters if you . . . love each other?"

"I can hardly expect you to understand," Hermione said scathingly, "but because I know I shall never get a better or more important offer than that of the Marquis, I am determined to become his wife."

"Will it make you happy to live so far away in Spain?" Valeda asked.

"I shall be the *Marquésa* de Silvana and the chatelaine of houses which I am told are finer than any of the Royal Palaces. The Marquis also has a house in Paris, and a Villa and estate in Italy."

She threw out her arms with a gesture that was very eloquent as she went on:

"He has everything! He is rich, important, and I want, as I have never wanted anything in my whole life, to be his wife!"

"Then I am sure, dearest," Valeda said, "you will succeed, but I cannot see how I can help you."

"That is just what I am going to tell you, and it is nothing very difficult. In fact, most women would jump at the idea."

"The idea of what?"

"Of coming with me to Spain."

The answer was so unexpected that Valeda gave a little gasp, then stared at Hermione as she went on:

"There is something else I have not told you, but which I am certain will clinch the matter once and for all."

"And . . . what is . . . that?" Valeda managed to gasp.

"I learnt last week, just before the Marquis went home, that my husband had invested in an oil-field in America. It was considered of no importance when his will was read. In fact, I remember the Solicitors saying they thought the shares were worthless and had therefore not been taken into account when assessing his estate."

Hermione paused for breath before she went on:

"Now, to everybody's astonishment, the oil-field has turned out to be one of the richest in the whole of Texas!"

Valeda waited, not fully understanding what this implied.

"My husband had left half his shares to our daughter,

Mirabelle, and the other half to me. They were in a codicil to his will, and as everybody was so sure that the investment was worthless, the Solicitors did not even mention it to me until a week ago."

She drew in her breath before she added:

"Now, as I understand it, Mirabelle and I are worth many millions of dollars! In fact, we are both very, very rich!"

"How wonderful! I am so happy for you!" Valeda cried.

"I cannot believe that such a tremendous sum of money would not influence the Marquis," Hermione said as if she spoke to herself. "No one, however rich he may be, would not be glad to welcome more!"

There was a short silence until Valeda said in a very small voice:

"You did say you wanted . . . me to come with you to . . . Spain?"

"Yes, yes, of course," Hermione said. "I am trying to tell you about it. When the Marquis asked me to visit his family, he included Mirabelle in the invitation because his sister has a little girl of exactly the same age."

She paused before she added:

"Of course, I accepted with alacrity because I was sure that he wanted his family to see Mirabelle as well as me."

Valeda thought privately that it was a rather uncomfortable way of being assessed.

She longed to ask what would happen if the Marquis's family did not think Hermione good enough for him, while he still loved her.

She, however, said nothing, and after a moment Hermione went on:

"It was all arranged that we should leave next Monday, when Mirabelle's Governess, who is really more of a Nanny, because after all Mirabelle is only six, refused to go with us because her mother is ill, or something equally tiresome!"

Once again there was that hard note in Hermione's voice which meant that she was annoyed at being thwarted in such a way.

Valeda was staring at her open-mouthed.

"Are you . . . suggesting—" she asked after a moment.

"I am saying," Hermione interrupted sharply, "that this is an opportunity for you to leave this dull ditchwater of a place and see a bit of the world. You can come with me to Spain and make yourself useful by looking after Mirabelle."

"But . . . will not the Marquis's family think that a little odd?"

"Not if they do not know who you really are," Hermione replied. "I would not be such an idiot as to take my sister with me as no more than a servant."

"Then . . . I do not . . . understand . . ."

"Try to be a little intelligent about it!" Hermione snapped. "I am offering you the chance of a lifetime. You will see the Royal Family of Spain and a great deal of the country."

She thought Valeda looked indecisive and said angrily:

"Heaven knows, you and Papa used to drone on about the wonder and beauty of other lands, and it will all cost you nothing."

Valeda was silent because she could not think of anything to say, and Hermione continued:

"We will think of some sensible name for you, and I am sure, as you will be looking after Mirabelle, that you will be very comfortable in the Nursery or School-Room."

Then as if she realised that her sister did not appear to be sharing her enthusiasm she asked:

"What is wrong? Why are you silent?"

"I am trying to understand why you are asking me," Valeda replied, "instead of trying to get, as I am sure you easily could, another ordinary Governess for Mirabelle."

"I can answer that quite simply," Hermione replied. "I can trust you not to talk."

She saw the surprise in Valeda's eyes and she explained:

"Do not be so half-witted, Valeda! If I engage a temporary Governess about whom I know nothing and who will leave me to go to another family in the same social sphere, she might talk."

"Talk about what?" Valeda asked in bewilderment.

"About me, of course!" Hermione said. "You do not suppose that there are not a hundred women who hate me because they are jealous of me? And one thing that would really delight them would be to learn that I wanted to marry the Marquis, but he did not ask me."

Sarcastically she added:

"It would be a story that would fly around Mayfair on the very wind, and I would be made to look a fool!"

Valeda drew in her breath.

"Now I . . . understand."

"It is not very difficult," Hermione said, "for I would certainly not expect my sister to gossip about me. Anyway, when we return, you will come back here where there is no one to gossip with except the chickens and ducks!"

She gave a little laugh as if she had said something funny, then went on:

"But you will have a journey to remember, and, as I have already said, Valeda, there is no one I can trust in the present circumstances except you. I am sure you could not be so unkind as not to help me."

Just for a moment it flashed through Valeda's mind that she would like to refuse; to say that her sister was asking of her something degrading and at the same time hurtful.

Then she told herself that however humiliating the offer might seem, Hermione was genuinely asking for help, genuinely relying on her because there was no one else she could trust.

She drew in her breath, and then in a very low voice which seemed somehow unlike her own, she said:

"If I am really . . . important to you, Hermione . . . then of course . . . I will agree to anything you suggest."

"Good!" Hermione said.

There was, however, a note in her voice and an expression in her eyes that quickly told Valeda that she had had no intention of taking "no" for an answer and would have fought resolutely for what she wanted.

There was an interruption when the door opened and Banks came into the room to arrange a small gate-legged table in front of the sofa on which Valeda was sitting.

Then he brought in a silver tea-tray that they used only when there were visitors, on which there was the silver tea-pot, kettle, milk-jug, and sugar basin, all of which had been in the Alcester family for over a hundred years.

Valeda was aware of what an effort it had been for Mrs. Banks, who was even older than her husband, to cut the tiny sandwiches and to set out on a Crown Derby plate the remains of a Madeira cake which she had made earlier in the week.

There were also a few macaroons which should have been eaten several days ago and which Valeda was certain were now too hard to be enjoyable.

But at least the table was full and she hoped Hermione would not be too critical.

When Banks had left the room, Hermione said:

"The same old things for tea that we used to have when we were children! I cannot think how you can stand it! In London my French Chef is a superlative pastry-maker, and in the country the products of the Still-Room are quite famous!"

Then a shadow passed over Hermione's face which told Valeda that she was remembering she was no longer mistress of Eltsley Court, which was now in the hands of the new holder of the title.

Quickly to pass over the embarrassing moment Valeda said:

"Do have a sandwich. They are made of watercress which I know was picked only this morning."

"I do not want anything to eat," Hermione replied. "I have to be careful of my figure, but I would like a cup of tea if it is not too strong."

Valeda handed it to her, rising from the sofa to do so, and as Hermione took it and the rings on her fingers glinted in the sunlight she said a little tentatively:

"I . . . I am afraid you may not . . . approve of the . . . clothes I should have to . . . take with me . . . and there is very little time to . . . buy any more."

"I have already thought of that," Hermione answered. "I assure you, Valeda, in the position I have held all these years I have learnt to be a good organiser and leave nothing to chance."

"I am sure you are very efficient."

"I am, and that is why I have already chosen a number of gowns which you will be able to wear in Spain and which I hope will not appear too elaborate for a Governess."

The way she said the last few words made Valeda press her lips together as if to prevent herself from saying that after all she had changed her mind and would not do what her sister wanted.

But Hermione went on:

"I told my maid to remove any unnecessary frills and furbelows on the gowns, and as I remember you always used to be very good at sewing, while I hated it. I am sure you can make any other alterations yourself that are really necessary."

"Y-yes . . . of course . . ."

"You will find bonnets, hats, and anything else that is necessary in the trunk, which I expect has already been packed," Hermione continued. "But for goodness' sake, Valeda, do something about your hair and make yourself look tidy, as a Governess should."

She spoke with a sharp note in her voice, then as she looked at her sister there was a different expression in her eyes from what had been in them before.

It was almost as if she were looking at her for the first time, and after what seemed to Valeda to be a long and uncomfortable scrutiny, she said slowly:

"Perhaps I am making a mistake and I would really be better advised to find somebody older and a good deal uglier than you."

Then as if she told herself she was being needlessly apprehensive she said:

"Oh, what does it matter what you look like? The Spaniards are as proud as the devil and would not be interested in anyone who is to them a servant and, of course, a completely inferior being!"

"Perhaps it would be better if I did not come with you!" Valeda said. "I dare say Nanny could manage the journey. She is over sixty-five but still quite spry, and you can trust her."

She thought as she spoke that she was being rather stupid in throwing away what, as Hermione had said, was a unique opportunity.

At the same time, if the Spaniards had their pride, she had hers.

Unexpectedly Hermione laughed.

"Now you are taking umbrage," she said, "which is what I used to do when I was young."

She rose to her feet as she spoke and put her arm around her sister's shoulders.

"I want you to come with me," she said in a conciliatory voice, "and it will be fun because we will be able to talk together quite frankly, and probably very indiscreetly about the Spaniards."

She was being so unexpectedly affectionate that Valeda felt the tears come into her eyes, and she knew that although she had tried not to do so, she had always missed her older sister.

"And you will be able to warn me if you think I am making a mistake," Hermione was saying. "After all, Carlos, however puffed up he may be with his own consequence, is not the only man in the world, and now that I am so rich, there will be even more men than there were before kneeling at my feet and beseeching me to give them what they want."

She looked so lovely as she spoke that Valeda found herself saying:

"How could anybody refuse you anything, Hermione, when you are so beautiful?"

"There might be a first time," Hermione retorted, "and that would definitely be a mistake!"

chapter two

AFTER that everything happened so quickly that Valeda thought she must be in a dream.

Hermione finished her cup of tea with a somewhat wry expression on her face, as if it were not good enough for her, and she said:

"Now you had better hurry because I want to get back to the house where I am staying before it is dark, and we leave very early tomorrow morning for London."

"You mean me to come with you?" Valeda asked.

"Of course! There is no point in your not doing so," Hermione replied. "I am staying with a very old relation of Arthur's who is almost blind. I shall tell her you are my sister, but after that you become Mirabelle's new Governess whom I am taking to London with me."

The way she spoke told Valeda she had had it all mapped out in her mind before she arrived. She knew

that her sister was so determined that whatever her incli-
nation had been she would eventually have given in to
Hermione's demands.

She suddenly felt helpless and as if she were stepping
into a strange world about which she knew nothing.

"What shall I pack?" she asked.

"Nothing!" Hermione replied. "You will find everything you need in London, including nightgowns and
underclothes for which I have no further use, and I am
sure my maid has even remembered you would want a
hair-brush."

Perceptively she was aware that Valeda was going to
ask her a question, and before she could form it on her
lips Hermione went on:

"My lady's-maid is in fact the only person who will
know who you are, and why you are with me. She has
been with me ever since I married and adores me, so I
can trust her as I can trust *nobody else!*"

She emphasised the last words sharply, and Valeda
was aware they were a kind of warning.

Bemused, and finding it hard to think out everything
clearly, she went upstairs and put on her best gown and
cloak which she had had since just before her father
died and had been quite expensive.

When she came downstairs again, she thought that
Hermione looked at her disparagingly.

At the same time she said nothing, except that they
should hurry, as she was sure the horses were growing
restless.

"Not that it will hurt them, considering how little
they have to do," she added.

"I thought they must be yours because no one I know
has such a smart carriage," Valeda said.

"If you call that smart," Hermione said, "wait until you see what is in my stable. When I drive in the Park, everybody turns to look not only at me, but at my horses, my carriage, and my servants!"

She was boasting, Valeda thought, just as she had done at home, when she always insisted that anything she owned was better than anybody else's.

"I shall look forward to seeing them," Valeda replied.

"We must stop talking and get started!" Hermione said sharply. "I have masses of things to do in London before we leave for Spain, and the sooner you settle down and make yourself pleasant to Mirabelle, the better!"

She hardly allowed her sister time to tell the servants she was going away or to instruct old Abbey to look after the horses before they were driving away down the road.

As Valeda looked back at the Manor House she had the uncomfortable feeling that she was making a mistake in leaving home and would far better have stayed where she was.

At the same time she could not help being excited at the thought of travelling, even if under somewhat unusual circumstances.

'I am sure this is something you want me to do, Papa,' she said silently to her father.

It was almost as if she could hear his voice telling her of the beauties of Madrid and the splendour of the Royal Palace which now she would be able to see with her own eyes.

When they reached, after a long drive, the house where Hermione was staying, she was surprised to find that the old cousin who was the late Earl's relative was the Dowager Duchess of Wantage.

The house was a large, rambling mansion, bigger than any house Valeda had ever visited before.

The Dowager Duchess greeted her very kindly.

"So you are Hermione's sister," she said. "Are you as beautiful as she is?"

"I am afraid not, Ma'am," Valeda replied. "While she looks like a perfect English rose, I am an ordinary little daisy whom nobody notices."

The Dowager Duchess chuckled.

"I suspect," she said, "that you are being over-modest, and if I cannot use my eyes, there is nothing wrong with my ears. So I can tell you one thing, my dear, you have a very beautiful voice."

"It is kind of you to say so," Valeda replied, "because in that case I am like my mother, who made everything she said sound like a poem and she could sing, my father always said, like a lark."

The Dowager Duchess laughed, and Valeda thought she was just going to talk about her mother when Hermione came back into the room and said sharply:

"I hope, Cousin Louise, my sister is not boring you. I am afraid she has lived so long in the country that she has little to talk about except the birds and the rabbits."

Knowing Hermione, Valeda realised she was not deliberately being rude, but warning her not to say too much to the Dowager Duchess.

She could not imagine any reason why she should be secretive about her family.

Then she suspected that Hermione, having on her marriage disappeared into a different world from the one in which she had been born, had doubtless invented for herself a largely fictitious background.

This suspicion was confirmed later, when as they went up to bed, having dined alone because the Dowager Duchess retired early, Hermione said:

"You are not likely to meet any more of Arthur's relatives as my sister. But if you do, I do not want you to talk about our home or about Papa and Mama."

"Why not?" Valeda asked bluntly.

There was just a pause while Hermione was feeling for words. Then she said:

"If you want the truth, I have no wish for people to know that I came from such a dull and unimportant background."

Valeda laughed.

What you are telling me, Hermione, is that you thought up a glamorous fairy-story in which you were the Princess and the Manor House a Palace."

Just for a moment Hermione looked a little disconcerted. Then she, too, laughed.

"You are right," she said. "I did embroider a little on my background. But make no mistake, Valeda, I intend to live in Palaces from now on."

"Is that the real reason why you want to marry the Marquis?"

"It certainly makes him more attractive than he is anyway," Hermione admitted. "Eltsley Court was palatial, and, although it is no longer mine, I have every intention of seeing that any house that takes its place is just as large and magnificent."

They had both walked into Hermione's bedroom as they were talking and she moved across the room to stand in front of the large mirror.

Her reflection in her evening-gown with a necklace

of turquoise and diamonds encircling her long neck made her look, Valeda thought, so beautiful that she was quite certain Hermione would obtain everything she desired, and so much more.

She was just about to say so when her sister said:

"Look at me! How could any man not want to have a wife who is so beautiful at the end of his table, and a wife who is also a millionairess?"

She gave a cry of sheer delight as she said:

"I am rich! Really enormously rich, Valeda! I can buy for myself anything I want without having to plead with some man to be generous to me."

"I am sure that is something you would never have to do," Valeda remarked.

Hermione considered for a moment before she said:

"Arthur was generous when it suited him, but at other times he could be what I considered really mean."

She paused, then went on:

"The Christmas before he died, for instance, I asked him for a chinchilla cape and two long ropes of pearls."

"It sounds rather a lot!" Valeda murmured.

"He refused to give me the cape," Hermione continued as if she had not spoken, "with the excuse that my ermine one was very becoming and was only two years old."

She turned from the mirror and with a little lilt in her voice cried:

"Now I can buy all the chinchillas I want for myself and I can make sure, Valeda, that there is no woman in the whole length and breadth of England as well dressed as I shall be."

Hermione was still talking of the things she could buy for herself when Valeda kissed her good night and went to her own room.

Only when she was alone did it strike her that never once had her sister suggested spending her money on anything or anyone else but herself.

She could not help reflecting, although it felt slightly disloyal, that if it had been her mother who had inherited so much money, there would have been hundreds of people who would have benefitted by it too.

There was no one in the village or in the neighbourhood who, if they were ill, would not find Lady Alcester at their bedside.

She took them herbal potions that she had distilled herself from the herb-garden of the Manor or, if they were poor, nourishing soup and other food which would tempt an invalid.

Good-natured though her father was, Valeda could remember him remonstrating with her mother that she would give away her last gown as well as his shirt if there were many more beggars knocking on their back-door.

"But I feel so sorry for them, darling," Lady Alcester would explain. "Those who came today have been walking, they tell me, for over two weeks, as they are going to live with their parents in Worcester, and the children are so tired. I feel sure they have not had a decent meal for days."

When the family, who had slept in the barn, left the next morning at dawn, they took with them two hens and any eggs on which they could lay their hands. Lady Alcester merely said when this was reported to her, with some indignation:

"Poor things! Well, at least they will not go hungry for a day or so."

It was her mother, Valeda remembered, who kept in touch with all their distant relations who, because they lived far away and it was impossible to visit them except very occasionally, felt neglected.

Until Valeda was sixteen her father had tried to carry on because he knew it was what her mother would wish.

Then he had handed her the latest bundle of letters they had written, saying:

"You answer these, my dear, I find them rather a bore."

Valeda had at first sympathised with him, especially when a great number of the letters were begging for money in one way or another.

Sometimes it was for a special charity or local interest; others would be pleas for loans which she was quite sure would never be repaid.

Her father had done what he could for those who he admitted were less fortunate than himself, but he was not a rich man.

In fact, he and his wife, when she was alive, had been so generous that they often had to cut back their own expenses, which usually meant that a horse on which her father had his eye went to another purchaser.

"I am sure Hermione will help other people now that she is so rich," Valeda told herself before she went to sleep.

Then she had the feeling that one person she was sure would not benefit from her sister's wealth was herself.

* * *

The next morning they left for London, but before they did so, Valeda went to say goodbye to the Dowager Duchess in her bedroom, for she was too old and ill to get up early.

"I have loved having you here, my dear," she said,

"and I hope you will come again."

Valeda was surprised, and involuntarily she replied:

"Do you really mean that, Ma'am?"

"I mean it in all sincerity," the Dowager Duchess replied, "and my maid tells me that you are very lovely, lovelier in her eyes, at any rate, than your sister!"

Valeda laughed.

"That is complete nonsense!" she said. "Hermione, I am sure, is the most beautiful person in the whole of England, and the newspapers always refer to her as 'The Beautiful Countess.'"

"Well, I am content with your beautiful voice, my dear," the Dowager Duchess said. "So come and see me again, and I shall be very disappointed if you do not permit yourself to return."

On an impulse Valeda bent and kissed the Dowager Duchess's cheek.

"Thank you," she said, "I am very touched by what you have just said to me, and I would love to come again."

Hermione had borrowed from the Duchess the carriage in which she arrived at the Manor so that her horses could rest before the return journey to London.

Now as they drove away in her own carriage she said:

"Well, it was useful to be able to stay with the old Dowager. At the same time, I hope the next place I rest my head will not prove so exceedingly boring."

"I found it very interesting," Valeda said.

"I suppose that was in contrast to the deadliness of home," Hermione replied rather rudely. "If I had to stay at the Manor for long, I should expect soon to look like a turnip, and and be about as exciting as one!"

Valeda tried not to feel hurt at hearing her home being disparaged, and to change the subject she encouraged Hermione to tell her about the things she wished to buy.

"Of course, I might purchase a large and impressive house near London," she said reflectively, "where I could give enormous parties. I believe there are quite a number of impoverished aristocrats ready to sell their ancestral mansions to the highest bidder."

"It sounds rather exciting," Valeda said.

"But if I marry somebody who already has a large house, it would be unnecessary and, if I marry the Marquis, as I intend to do, I shall be spending most of my life abroad."

"Are you quite certain, now that you are so rich, that you want to marry him?" Valeda asked.

"I find him very attractive," Hermione said, "and as I have already told you, there is no one more important, unless I marry Royalty, and I suppose that is impossible."

"I have always understood that Royal blood is matched with Royal blood," Valeda remarked, "and the Queen upholds that principle."

Hermione gave a little sigh as if she felt it was frustrating that she could not become a Royal Princess.

"Of course I would like to be a Duchess," she said, "but there is only one unmarried Duke, and he is so old and unpleasant that I could not contemplate him for an instant!"

"I am sure he would want to marry you," Valeda said.

"A great many men want to do that," Hermione remarked complacently. "I have decided, however, that I would rather be the *Marquésa* de Silvala than anything else, and that, my dear Valeda, is why we are going to Spain!"

* * *

Hermione's house in London was, as Valeda had expected, large, very well furnished, and situated in the fashionable and exclusive Park Lane.

The windows overlooked Hyde Park, and when she looked out of her window and saw the trees, their branches moving a little in the evening breeze, she had a sudden vision of the woods at home.

Once again she thought perhaps she was making a mistake in leaving them.

From the moment they arrived, Hermione began speaking to her in a different voice from the one she had used before, and she said to the Butler:

"This is Miss Warde, the new Governess for Lady Mirabelle. See that somebody shows her upstairs."

"Very good, M'Lady," the Butler replied, and deputed a smartly liveried young footman to do what was required.

As Valeda followed him up the stairs, leaving Hermione below in the hall, she had the feeling that a barrier had been thrown up between herself and her sister. She was now alone in a very different way, although she had been alone at home.

The Housekeeper, rustling in black silk, introduced herself as Mrs. Winterton and led her to the Nurseries, which were very spacious and on the second floor.

As Valeda entered the room which contained a rocking-horse, a large dolls'-house and a brass-edged guard in front of the fire, she thought she might be stepping back in years. It was exactly how her own Nursery had looked when she was a child.

A young housemaid rose as they entered and a small girl, elaborately dressed in a frilly frock with a blue sash, came running towards the Housekeeper with a doll in her arms.

"Look, Mrs. Winty," she said, which was the nearest she could get to Winterton, "poor little Emma has cracked her face!"

"So she has, M'Lady," Mrs. Winterton said, looking down at the doll. "But don't you worry, we'll get someone to take her to the Dolls' Hospital and have a new head put on her."

"You did not give me a new head when I scratched my face," Mirabelle said.

Then as she suddenly realised the Housekeeper was not alone, she looked at Valeda enquiringly.

"This is Miss Warde, M'Lady," Mrs. Winterton said, "who's come to take the place of poor Miss Graham. Now shake hands and say that you are pleased to see her."

Valeda did not, however, wait, but crouching down so that her face was on a level with Mirabelle's, she said:

"Tell me about Emma, your doll. I had one very like her when I was your age, but she was called Tiddli-winks!"

Mirabelle laughed.

"That was a funny name!"

"I gave all my dolls funny names."

"I will show you my dolls," Mirabelle said.

Taking Valeda by the hand, she drew her across the room to where, seated along a shelf by the dolls'-house,

36

there were over a dozen dolls, each one exquisitely dressed and having real hair.

By the time Valeda had inspected them, the House-keeper had tactfully withdrawn from the Nursery.

"Will you show me where I am to sleep?" Valeda asked. "It will be only for one night, because tomorrow we are going to Spain."

"That is what Mama said," Mirabelle replied, "but I do not think I want to go to Spain. Betty said they fight bulls and all the food tastes of oil."

Valeda guessed that Betty was the maid who had been looking after her, and she said:

"I do not want to go to a bull-fight, but I believe that Spain is very beautiful, and it will be interesting to see them dancing and clicking their castanets as they do so."

She had to explain what castanets were, and by the time she had finished, Mirabelle was looking forward to seeing Spain and talked about it all the time Valeda was putting her to bed.

"Does your Mama come upstairs to say good night to you?" Valeda asked. "Or do you go down to her?"

"Sometimes I go down," Mirabelle replied, "but not when there's a lot of people there."

Valeda did not speak, and she went on:

"The gentlemen, who Betty says all love Mama be-cause she is so beautiful, kiss me, and their moustaches tickle my cheeks."

Valeda laughed and said:

"I agree that is rather tiresome, but I hope your mother will be coming to see you tonight."

Mirabelle shrugged her shoulders in a way which told Valeda without words that it was very unlikely.

Then, having eaten a supper of scrambled eggs and a large glass of milk, Mirabelle said her prayers while Valeda listened and then tucked her up in bed.

"Good night, dear," Valeda said softly. "Tomorrow I will think of some stories about Spain to tell you so that you will know a little about it before we get there."

"I would like that," Mirabelle said. "Do you know lots and lots of stories?"

"Yes, lots," Valeda replied.

She was thinking of those both her father and mother had told her all her life, and how she could make them understandable to this small but very intelligent little girl.

"That will be fun," Mirabelle said. "I am glad you have come to look after me. Miss Graham never knew any stories in her head, but read them out of a book. So they did not sound like proper stories, but more like lessons."

Valeda kissed her again.

"My stories are all real stories," she said, "and when we get to Spain, you will be able to see if what I have told you is right or wrong."

"If they are wrong, you will have some very bad marks!" Mirabelle laughed.

As Valeda turned out the light and shut the door, she thought her new charge was a very attractive one.

At the same time, she thought it a mistake that the child had been left so much with servants and a Governess who did not sound more than just adequate.

She obviously lacked what she herself had known in her own childhood, the love of an adoring mother and father. But she knew this was something she could not say to Hermione.

While she was thinking about her sister, she wondered if there was any chance of seeing her again that evening.

The answer to that was quite positive when her supper was brought up to the Nursery on a tray, and there was no message asking her to go downstairs to see Hermione.

When Betty, who she learned was the nurserymaid, came to draw the curtains, Valeda could not help asking if Her Ladyship was dining in.

"Ow, yes, Miss!" Betty replied. "She's got one of her 'special gentlemen' to dinner."

Valeda must have looked surprised, because Betty explained:

"That's wot we calls the gentlemen as comes 'ere frequent. There's ever so many of them, and one or two are favourites, so to speak."

Valeda felt it was a mistake to discuss her employer with one of the servants, but Betty chatted on:

"You should've seen the mistress goin' down to dinner. Looking beautiful, she was! She 'ad on a new gown of pale green, sparklin' all over with sequins an' emeralds round her neck."

"It sounds very grand!" Valeda managed to say.

"I 'spects Her Ladyship an' the gentleman as is here for dinner will go on to a Ball," Betty said with relish. "That's wot her lady's-maid thought they'd be doing because Her Ladyship was wearin' her emerald tiara."

Valeda could not help wondering what she would have felt if, just for one night, Hermione had offered to take her as her sister to a Ball in London.

It was something her mother had often talked about after Hermione had married.

"It is the luckiest thing that ever happened that Hermione should have stayed in London during the Season and met her future husband the first week she arrived."

Lady Alcester had sighed with satisfaction and added:

"That is what must happen to you, my darling, in a few years time."

"It sounds thrilling, Mama," Valeda had said, "although I should hate to go away from you and Papa, and, of course, the horses."

"I hope one day," Lady Alcester went on, "you will have a home of your own as Hermione has now, and your husband will see that you have good horses to ride."

Lady Alcester had often referred, as time passed, to the invitation which had changed her elder daughter's life, even though she regretted seeing so little of her.

"Why does Hermione never come home, Mama?" Valeda had asked at first, before she realised it was a question that hurt her mother and brought an expression of pain to her beautiful eyes.

"I expect, dearest, she has a very good reason for having to stay with her husband," Lady Alcester replied, "and in the glamorous world in which she now lives, we must seem very dull by comparison."

Valeda had vowed to herself that if ever she married, however much she might be in love with her husband, she would never let her mother and father feel neglected.

"One thing is quite certain," she told herself resolutely when she went to bed in the room that led off the Nursery, "I shall be expected to keep my place as Mirabelle's Governess whether I am here or in Madrid."

As she turned out the light she knew that she did not

mind so much the inferior position of being a Governess to suit Hermione, but the fact that her sister had no love for her.

She had brought her back into her life simply to suit her own purpose, which was to marry the Marquis de Silvala.

*　　*　　*

The following day was a bustle from the first thing in the morning, when Betty called her, until she finally fell asleep with the wheels of a *wagon-lit* rumbling beneath her.

With the help of both Betty and Mrs. Winterton, she and Mirabelle had dressed, eaten their breakfast, and were downstairs waiting in the hall at exactly nine o'clock.

There was an immense amount of luggage to be put into one carriage which, when it was full, drove off with the Courier who was to escort them to Spain and with him Miss Jones, her sister's lady's-maid.

It was she whom Hermione had told her she could trust, and who was the only person who knew Valeda's real identity.

Valeda had had a brief encounter with her as she waited in the hall and thought she looked plain and slightly disagreeable, but with an obvious awareness that she was of great importance to her mistress.

She said goodbye to Mrs. Winterton in a slightly condescending tone, who had then introduced her to Valeda.

"This is Miss Warde, who's taken Miss Graham's place in looking after Her little Ladyship," Mrs. Winterton said.

Miss Jones inclined her head.

"I hope you'll be happy with us—Miss Warde."

There was a perceptible pause before she said the name.

"I am sure I shall," Valeda replied, "and I am looking forward to seeing Spain."

Miss Jones sniffed.

"I never was one for them foreign parts."

Without saying any more, she went through the front door and into the carriage that was already piled with trunks.

Valeda guessed that the man accompanying her was their Courier, simply because he looked like one, but she had no chance to ask his name, for down the stairs came a vision of beauty.

Hermione's travelling-gown of dark blue satin covered with a cloak edged with sable was elegant beyond words, as was the bonnet to match, which was trimmed with flowers and velvet ribbons.

As she reached the hall Mrs. Winterton dropped her a curtsy, and the footmen bowed.

"Good-morning, Mirabelle!" Hermione said to her daughter, who ran towards her. "I hope you are going to be very good on what will be a long journey."

"I am going to be good because all the way Miss Warde is going to tell me stories about Spain," Mirabelle replied.

Just for a moment the eyes of the two sisters met. Then Hermione turned away, saying in her sharp voice:

"Come along, what are we waiting for? It would be a great mistake to miss the train!"

She moved like a ship in full sail out through the front door and into the second carriage.

Valeda, knowing what was expected of her, took

Mirabelle's hand and followed.

"Goodbye, Mrs. Winterton," she said in a low voice.

"Goodbye, Miss Warde, and enjoy yourself," Mrs. Winterton replied, "and may your journey be a safe one."

"I am sure it will be that." Valeda smiled.

A footman helped Mirabelle into the carriage where she sat beside her mother while Valeda sat opposite her with her back to the horses.

They set off and Mirabelle waved until those standing on the doorstep were out of sight.

Then she sat back and said:

"I wanted to bring all my dolls with me, but Miss Warde says you will buy me some Spanish ones in Madrid."

"I expect that will be possible," Hermione replied, "and I know there will be some children you will meet when we get there who will share their toys with you."

"I want my own dolls!" Mirabelle said, pouting for a moment.

"I have packed two of them," Valeda said quickly, "and they are nice and comfortable for the journey, so I think you had better let them rest until we reach Madrid."

"Of course she can wait until we get to Madrid!" Hermione said crossly. "For goodness' sake, Valeda, do not spoil the child! She has to do as she is told, and not make a nuisance of herself. If there is one thing I cannot stand, it is tiresome children!"

The way Hermione spoke was so severe that Valeda looked at her in surprise, but Mirabelle took it as a matter of course and only slipped across the carriage to sit beside Valeda.

"Can I have a story now, Miss Warde?" she asked coaxingly.

"I think we had better wait until we are in the train," Valeda replied. "There will be plenty of time then to tell stories and play a guessing game I used to play when I was a little girl."

"What was that?" Mirabelle asked, intrigued.

"My father and mother taught it to my sister and to me," Valeda explained. "When we drove about the countryside, we would see people and try to guess what they did. If they were strange-looking or unusual in any way, my mother would tell us a story about them."

As she spoke Valeda looked at Hermione, wondering if she remembered how much they had enjoyed the guessing game.

When they grew older, their mother or their father, whoever they were with, would encourage them to explain why they thought the person in question was a blacksmith, a farmer, a huntsman, or a poacher.

Then they would have to tell an imaginative story of what their lives were like.

To her it had been so enchanting and so fascinating that she could not believe that Hermione had forgotten it and would not wish her own child's imagination to be developed in the same manner.

But Hermione only looked out of the window and said:

"We are nearing the station. There is no time for games, and remember, Mirabelle, that you curtsy to my friends who will be seeing us off, and do not say anything impertinent to them."

There was something in the hard way she spoke which told Valeda she had no intention of remembering the past, or being in any way sentimental about it.

She knew then, if she had not known it before, that she had lost her sister completely.

She also knew that Hermione was very different from what she had been before she married.

As she felt a little pang of pain at the loss of something which had always been very precious, she felt Mirabelle put her small hand into hers.

Then she knew that if she had lost Hermione, she had found Mirabelle, and already her niece had crept into her heart.

chapter three

WHEN they reached Calais, it was very exciting for Valeda to find there was a private coach exactly like the one, someone said proudly, used by Queen Victoria, attached to the train which was to carry them through France to Spain.

Mirabelle was thrilled and ran about saying it was a little house on wheels, until Hermione crossly told her to keep quiet.

Then she settled down beside Valeda, saying:

"Please, Miss Warde, tell me a lovely story about a little house on wheels."

"I will think of one," Valeda promised. "In the meantime, let us talk about the Spanish people we are going to see, what they do, and what they look like."

After Mirabelle had gone to bed, Valeda had the chance of talking to her sister alone, and Hermione dropped her frigid air and became warm and confidential.

47

"I am glad you are here," she said, "for to tell you the truth, Valeda, I feel rather as if I were a parcel of goods on sale or return."

Valeda laughed.

"It must be disconcerting for you, when you are so beautiful and everybody looks on you as someone very, very special."

"That is what I want to believe," Hermione said with a little sigh, "but the Marquis is different."

"In what way is he different?" Valeda asked, hoping she would be told the truth.

Hermione hesitated a moment, then she said:

"I suppose one of the reasons why I find him so attractive is that in a way he is out of reach. He is so much grander, not only because of his rank, but simply in himself, than any other man who has paid court to me in London."

Valeda tried to understand what Hermione was saying and she went on:

"He gives one the impression that the world is made for him to walk on, and he also has a cynical twist to his lips, as if he thinks everyone he meets is trying to deceive him."

Valeda was astonished.

"Why should he think that?" she asked.

"I believe the answer," Hermione replied, "is that when he was very young he was married in the arranged fashion usual among Spanish noble families to a girl whose blood was as aristocratic and blue as his own. But from the moment they were married they hated each other."

"Surely they must have had some idea of that before they were actually man and wife?"

Hermione laughed.

"I see you have no conception how strictly chaperoned foreign girls are. Carlos told me once he never had a single conversation with his wife until they drove away from their wedding-reception and were alone."

"That is very unnatural," Valeda murmured, "and one can hardly expect anybody to be happy in such circumstances."

"It is what happens all over Europe," Hermione said lightly. "So I am sure that he is determined that his second marriage shall be a happy one—that is, if he finally decides to have another wife. His first died six years ago."

Valeda looked astonished.

"Are you telling me that you think he may, after all this, decide that he does not wish to marry you . . . or anyone . . . else?"

"It is a distinct possibility," Hermione said frankly, "but I am determined—yes, determined, Valeda—to be his wife!"

She made a little murmur that had something rapturous about it as she added:

"Think how important I shall be! All those women who have looked down their noses at me because they are jealous will have to 'eat humble pie,' and that is something I shall greatly enjoy watching!"

Valeda thought to herself that it was more important for Hermione to be concerned with whether or not the Marquis really loved her, but she did not say so.

She thought only that as Hermione was such a success in London, where there must be at least half-a-dozen distinguished suitors for her hand, it was a mistake to go rushing half across Europe in pursuit of an elusive Spaniard.

She did not, however, say this aloud, but merely encouraged her sister to go on talking.

"Of course I know Carlos would find it much easier if I consented to be his mistress, but that is something I have no intention of being!"

Valeda gave a cry of horror.

"Of course not! How could you do anything so wrong and wicked as to allow any man to make love to you unless you were married to him?"

She thought her sister looked at her in a somewhat strange way before she said rather hastily:

"Yes, of course, Valeda, you are right, and that is why I have kept Carlos at arm's length, which has surprised him."

"I should have thought it was something he might have expected from you," Valeda said a little stiffly.

Hermione laughed.

"All Spaniards are promiscuous and pursue any pretty woman, and they are certainly set an example for good or bad, whichever you like to call it, by their King."

"What do you mean?" Valeda asked.

"The stories about King Alfonso's infidelity are well known in London," Hermione answered, "but in this case I suppose it is understandable."

"Why?"

"I thought you were so good at history!" Hermione said in a sarcastic voice. "Surely you know that Alfonso the Twelfth was married in 1878 to the Infanta Mercedes who was the daughter of the Duke and Duchess of Montpensier."

"Yes, I do remember now," Valeda said in a low voice, but Hermione went on.

"Carlos said she was very beautiful, with huge dark

eyes and her hair was the true Andalusian black."

Hermione paused for a moment, then said with a touch of sharpness in her voice:

"He was, in fact, quite lyrical about her, saying she was a perfect prototype of Spanish womanhood, delicate and distinguished."

"I seem to remember now that she died."

"Yes, apparently it was a great tragedy," Hermione agreed. "They were married for only five months. It was a real love-match, and King Alfonso adored her."

"What a terrible thing to happen!" Valeda exclaimed. "Why did she die?"

"It was said to have been from gastric fever," Hermione replied, "and she died only two days after her eighteenth birthday. The King was so broken-hearted that they were afraid, Carlos tells me, his health would be destroyed."

"But he married again."

"Of course," Hermione answered. "It was expected of him in his position and he chose, I believe very wisely, the Arch-Duchess Maria Cristina of Hapsburg, a second cousin to the Emperor of Austria."

"But he is not happy with her?" Valeda asked, feeling suddenly very sorry for the young King she had not seen.

Hermione shrugged her shoulders.

"Apparently she makes him a very good Queen but, as he is not in love with her, he naturally amuses himself with some very attractive and charming women."

Valeda was astonished.

"Are you telling me that the King has . . . mistresses?" she asked in an outraged tone.

"Oh, really, Valeda!" Hermione said. "How can you

be so naïve and out of touch with reality. Of course he has mistresses, as his marriage was merely one of convenience."

"But . . . but it is . . . wrong!"

Hermione made an impatient sound.

"I cannot think that you did not learn a little bit about life from those dreary old books you and Papa were always browsing over even when you were a little girl!"

Her voice was scathing as she asked:

"Surely you realise that in the Social World in every country men marry women who are suitable for their position in life, usually chosen for them by their parents. You cannot expect them therefore not to amuse themselves as well."

Valeda was silent for a moment. Then she said:

"I cannot imagine anybody like Papa doing anything so wicked, and I am sure, dearest, if any man like the Marquis suggested anything like that to you, you would tell him how disgraceful you thought it was!"

Hermione got up suddenly from the seat on which they were sitting side by side and said sharply:

"I must go to bed! I want to look attractive when we arrive in Madrid, which is going to be very difficult after a long and tedious journey with really no one to talk to."

Valeda was hurt, but she did not say so.

She only thought she had been stupid in upsetting her sister when she had begun talking so warmly and confidentially to her.

When she was alone in her small compartment with the wheels of the train rumbling under her, she found herself thinking how strange it was that Hermione, who was her own mother's child, should find it quite acceptable that the King and apparently a lot of other men should be unfaithful to their wives.

"When I marry," she told herself in the darkness, "I want to marry a man who will love me . . . really love me . . . and will in consequence not find any other woman attractive!"

Then humbly she thought she was asking too much.

Perhaps men who moved in high-society were different from her father and, as Hermione had said, she was countrified and out of touch with reality.

As the train travelled on through the night, she found herself wishing she had stayed at home with the horses to ride happily over the fields and in the woods, content with her thoughts and her imagination.

"I made a mistake in agreeing to what Hermione asked," she decided.

Then she remembered that the trip to Spain would not last for ever, and she was sure there would be a great many delights to think about and remember once she returned home.

'At least I shall see the pictures in the Prado Museum,' she thought.

She remembered how her father had talked about them as one of the finest collections in the whole of Europe and described how beautiful they were.

"I will not think about the behaviour of the King, the Marquis, or any other man," she decided just before she fell asleep. "I will just look at what is beautiful and that memory will remain with me long after everything else is forgotten!"

*   *   *

It was, in fact, a long journey, and they more than once had to wait in a siding before the private coach could be attached to another train.

Nevertheless, Valeda managed to keep Mirabelle amused. Although it meant telling the child a great many stories, she found herself remembering ones she had long forgotten which brought back memories of her own childhood when Hermione had been at home.

That was a time when she had believed they had all been rapturously happy.

As they drew nearer and nearer to Madrid, Hermione grew more and more cross if anything went wrong, and she obviously found Mirabelle's chatter and high spirits irritating.

In an effort to pass the time, Valeda taught the little girl how to draw pictures of the people they saw in the stations at which they stopped, and of animals and birds in the countryside as they sped past them.

She found Mirabelle had quite an aptitude for drawing. That made it easier for her to tell her about the pictures in the Prado and the beauty of them, just as her father had described them to her in the past.

By the time they reached Madrid, Mirabelle was looking forward to seeing not only the people, of whom Valeda was rather apprehensive, but the buildings, the pictures, and the beauty of Spain itself.

Hermione spent hours dressing herself for their arrival. When the train drew into the station and Valeda had a quick sight of a number of distinguished-looking gentlemen awaiting them, she thought as her sister came from her bedroom that the effort had been worthwhile.

She certainly looked spectacular, the blue of her eyes being echoed in an elaborate gown trimmed with flowers of chiffon.

She wore a hat covered in ostrich feathers that fluttered as she walked and made her appearance even more sensational.

When the train came to a standstill, Hermione made no effort to alight, but stood in the centre of the Drawing-Room, waiting.

Holding Mirabelle's hand, Valeda kept in the background, feeling as if they were all taking part in a very strange play in which Hermione was the Leading Lady, and she and Mirabelle were very minor members of the cast.

At the same time she was extremely curious, and the first person to enter the Drawing-Room was, she knew without being told, the man they had come so far to see.

To say that the Marquis was magnificent was to understate his air of importance, and the fact was that the moment he appeared, everybody else seemed in some strange way to be dwarfed by him.

He was exceedingly handsome, and his dark eyes and dark hair would have proclaimed him anywhere in the world as a Spaniard.

At the same time, he had that indefinable air of good breeding that gave him an added distinction. It made Valeda sure it would be very difficult, if not impossible, to influence him, and he would always get his own way.

He walked towards Hermione without hurrying, and lifting her hand to his lips said:

"You are even more beautiful than I remember! Welcome to Spain, and on behalf of my country, may I say that everyone will be enriched by your presence?"

"It is wonderful to be here!" Hermione replied as she looked up at him.

Watching her, Valeda thought no one could be more

alluring or more lovely.

The Marquis was followed by several other men, whom he introduced as his cousins, and they kissed Hermione's hand and paid her extravagant compliments.

They all, Valeda noticed, spoke good English, with only a slight but very attractive accent.

Then, when the greetings were finished, the Marquis looked towards Valeda and Mirabelle, who were standing in the background.

"And how did your daughter enjoy the journey?" he asked Hermione.

"She was very good," Hermione replied. "Mirabelle, come and say 'how do you do.'"

Valeda gave the child a gentle push forward, and because she was well trained, she curtsied gracefully to the Marquis and the other gentlemen, who all began to make a fuss of her.

Valeda, as she watched what was happening, hoping that Mirabelle would please Hermione, was suddenly aware that the Marquis was looking at her in a penetrating manner with, she thought, an expression of surprise in his eyes.

After a moment he said:

"I do not think I have ever seen you before."

Valeda dropped him a curtsy, but before she could speak, Hermione said sharply:

"Miss Graham let me down at the last moment, and Miss Warde has taken her place."

She did not make it sound a particularly commendable action, and the Marquis moved to Hermione's side to say:

"All that matters is that you are here. My mother and sister are looking forward to seeing you, but first we are going to the Palace."

"To the Palace?" Hermione questioned.

"Yes, my sister is on duty as Lady-in-Waiting to Her Majesty, and since her little daughter is spending the day with the young Princesses, I thought we would go there first."

"That sounds delightful!" Hermione cried.

Valeda knew from the lilt in her voice that she was looking forward to meeting the King and Queen.

There were a number of carriages outside the station, and Valeda found herself driving alone with Mirabelle.

The Marquis's cousins were obviously determined to be with Hermione, while Miss Jones, the Courier, and the luggage had a large brake in which to travel direct to the Marquis's palace.

Valeda was thrilled that she could look out of the windows and see the wide streets lined with trees coming into bloom, and the fine houses, with their beautiful wrought-iron balconies, looking just as she had expected they would look.

Mirabelle was jumping up and down with excitement.

"We are going to the Palace to see the King and the Queen, Miss Warde!" she cried. "Will they be wearing their crowns?"

"I am afraid not, dearest."

Then there was so much to look at that even Mirabelle was silent.

The houses and Churches they were passing were, Valeda thought, breath-taking. But when they came to the Palace itself, she could find no words in which to describe it.

She had known, because her father had told her, that it had been built by the Bourbons and completed by Charles III.

Popularly known as the *Palacioa de Oriente* it occupied the same site on which once stood the old *Alcazar* of the House of Austria, which had been destroyed by fire.

It had taken twenty-six years to finish and, as they approached it, Valeda was well enough read to realise that the huge building had a French influence in its design.

Once she was inside she could only stare about her, thinking that no Palace could be more beautiful or a more fitting background for a King and Queen.

They climbed up the marble steps of the main staircase and were shown after walking through one Ante-Room after another into what she was to learn later was the *"Gasparini Room"* which had been decorated by the painter of that name.

The glorious painted ceiling, the huge chandeliers, the gold mirrors with lily lights in front of each one of them, were so breathtaking that Valeda could only stand and gasp.

She was aware that ahead of her Hermione was being presented to Queen Maria Cristina and standing beside her was the King.

Valeda was at first glance a little disappointed by Alfonso XII.

He was nothing as impressive-looking as the Marquis, but as she reached him, talking and smiling with Hermione, she realised he had an attractiveness, which was perhaps more important than dignity.

He had a clear, olive complexion and was fashionably moustached and bewhiskered, but she was sure it was his eyes that were his chief attraction.

They seemed to sparkle as they looked at Hermione,

and she thought her sister blossomed like a rose at the compliments he was paying her.

Then unexpectedly, so that Valeda started, the King asked in excellent English:

"And who is this charming young lady I see with the little girl who must be your daughter?"

Instantly Hermione stiffened, and she said in a deliberately cold and off-hand manner:

"That is just Mirabelle's Governess. I want Your Majesty to meet Mirabelle, who is greatly looking forward to seeing her first King."

King Alfonso laughed, and Valeda gently moved Mirabelle forward so that the child would go towards him and curtsy.

As she did so, King Alfonso said:

"I can see that one day you will be beautiful like your mother."

"Why are you not wearing your crown?" Mirabelle enquired.

Hermione turned her head with an angry expression in her eyes.

"I will show you my crown another day," King Alfonso promised, and Mirabelle said with a little skip of excitement:

"I would like that. Can I see it now?"

"His Majesty said another day, Mirabelle!"

As she spoke Hermione gave Valeda a meaningful look which told her she must prevent the child from making a nuisance of herself.

She moved forward obediently to take Mirabelle by the hand, but before she could do so the King asked:

"Is this your first visit to Spain?"

Valeda curtsied before she replied:

"Yes, Your Majesty, and it is very exciting for me."

"Then I hope you will not be disappointed."

She saw his dark eyes looking at her intently, and remembering the stories she had heard about him she could not help, although it annoyed her, feeling the blood come into her cheeks.

She would have moved away, but King Alfonso asked:

"What is your name?"

"Valeda . . . Warde, Your Majesty," she said, stumbling a little over the last name.

"A very pretty name for a very pretty person," the King said in a low voice.

Valeda hoped that Hermione had not heard his remark, but she saw with a sense of relief as she glanced at her sister that she was talking animatedly to the Queen and they were moving towards a sofa farther into the room.

Although she knew that Hermione had not heard the King's remark, she was sure that the Marquis had.

Without really meaning to, she looked towards him and thought that there was an expression of cynical contempt in his eyes, as if he thought she was deliberately trying to flirt with the King.

Embarrassed, she bent down to tighten the bow of Mirabelle's sash, and while she was doing so, the two men joined Hermione and the Queen.

A Lady-in-Waiting was ready to take Valeda and Mirabelle to join the Marquis's niece and the young Princesses in another part of the Palace.

While they were passing through one magnificent room after another, all Valeda wished was that her father were with her to explain the beautiful paintings, especially those by Velasquez, Rubens, Bassano, Watteau, and Vicente Lopez.

'I could spend a century here,' she thought to herself before they reached the rooms where they found the Marquis's niece, a dark-haired, attractive little girl the same age as Mirabelle, whose name was Francisca.

The Royal Princesses were too small to be of particular interest to Mirabelle, but their nurses enthused over her fair hair and blue eyes, and she was certainly a striking contrast to the other children.

A Lady-in-Waiting who was a shy, quiet woman said to Valeda:

"I am afraid you will find the Palace a little bewildering at first. I know when I came here I felt overwhelmed by it to such an extent that it frightened me."

"It is very beautiful," Valeda said. "I only hope I shall have time to see some of its treasures while we are staying in Madrid."

"I am sure you will," the Lady-in-Waiting replied, "since His Majesty is so fond of the Marquis that he likes to have him here every day if possible. His house, which is nearly as grand as this, is only a short distance away, so I am sure we shall see a lot of you and this dear little girl."

It was certainly something Valeda wanted.

They were told the carriage was waiting, and they walked back for what seemed a very long distance through connecting rooms to the main staircase, and she told herself she must try not to miss anything.

She must absorb the beauty of every picture, every piece of furniture, and every decorated ceiling while she was privileged to be in Madrid.

They drove to the Marquis's house, which was in

fact only about five minutes from the Palace, in two carriages, and once again Valeda and Mirabelle were alone.

They were to find as the Lady-in-Waiting had said, that the Marquis's house was no less impressive and, Valeda thought, even more beautiful, if that were possible, than the Palace.

It was very large and here, too, the furnishings, tapestries, and pictures could only be described as "magnificent."

By the time they reached the somewhat less grand but very comfortable bedrooms they were to occupy, Valeda thought she might have been walking in a dream.

Francisca's nurse was Spanish and she could not speak a word of English. It was a splendid opportunity for Valeda to find that the Spanish she had learned from her father made her not only able to understand what was said, but also to talk to the nurse and other servants.

They all exclaimed in delight and no longer thought of her as a foreigner, but as one of themselves.

"That is a compliment I really appreciate," she said.

Because they were happy and laughing, she began to enjoy herself, and not feel as nervous as she was with Hermione.

The children played together, and when they stopped for supper, Valeda found she was expected to eat with the Spanish nurse, and there was no chance of seeing Hermione that evening.

She was, however, tired and went to bed early to sleep peacefully and wake with a sense of excitement that she was actually in Madrid.

She had met the King and Queen and not only had

visited one Royal Palace, but judging from what she had seen of the Marquis's house, was living in another.

She learnt from Francisca's nurse that she and Mirabelle were expected to do anything they wished. So as soon as breakfast was finished and she had ascertained that Hermione did not wish to see Mirabelle, Valeda asked if she might take the child to the Prado Museum.

It was what she wanted to do herself, and she felt she must go there at once in case by some awful mischance she never had an opportunity of doing so again.

The Spanish Nanny told her it would be quite in order for her to ask for a carriage, and after putting a pretty muslin bonnet that matched her dress on Mirabelle's head, they set off.

Valeda felt in some way that she was playing truant, then told herself that no one would be in the least interested in what she and Mirabelle did.

The Prado was very impressive on the outside, as she had expected, and they climbed up a large number of steps to the entrance.

Because Valeda had been clever enough to make Mirabelle interested beforehand in seeing the pictures, she ran from one to another.

She exclaimed in delight at the funny little animals in Bosch's *The Garden of Delights* and was intrigued by the story of *Nastagio degli Honesti* as painted by Botticelli.

As they moved through the rooms, Valeda tried to find the picture that she thought would be of particular interest to a small girl, until she stopped in front of *Virgin and Child* by Luis de Morales.

It was a very lovely picture of the Virgin holding on her knee the child Jesus, who had slipped His hand into her gown to feel for her breast, and she looks down at him with an indescribable tenderness.

Valeda did not know why—in fact she had never heard of the picture before—but she felt a strange and compelling attraction to it.

She was telling herself it was because of its delicate technique and she knew that Morales had been called *The Divine One*.

At the same time there was something else she was subconsciously aware of, and she was wondering what it could be when she heard a deep voice behind her say:

"I somehow expected that you would find your way to this picture!"

Valeda gave a start and turned to find the Marquis standing just behind her. She was so astonished at his being there that it took her a moment before she hastily dropped him a curtsy.

"I saw you and Mirabelle coming into the Museum," he said, "and thought you were starting early on your sight-seeing tour."

"There is so much to see, My Lord," Valeda replied, "that I felt if we did not start quickly, we might have to go home before I have seen everything."

The Marquis laughed, and for a moment it swept away the cynical expression on his face and made him look much younger.

"You will certainly have to stay for a very long time to see everything in Madrid," he said. "But as I have said, I thought you would find your way to this picture."

The way he spoke seemed to have some special significance about it, and Valeda looked at him a little perplexed, then again at the picture.

"Surely you realise why it is attracting you?" he asked.

"I . . . I was thinking," Valeda said a little hesitatingly, "how beautifully painted it is."

"And what else?" the Marquis insisted.

She could not understand what he was suggesting, and looking at the picture once more she saw, as her father would have wanted her to do, a kind of halo of mystery around the Virgin's oval face, and a brilliantly painted, almost transparent veil which partially covered her hair.

But this did not quite explain the Marquis's attitude, and as she looked at him enquiringly, he said:

"I think, Miss Warde, that you can never have looked in a mirror!"

Valeda's eyes widened. Then she stammered a little incoherently:

"Are . . . are you saying . . . My Lord . . . ?"

Even as she spoke she knew he was right. There was, although it seemed impossible, an unmistakable resemblance between her own face and the one in the picture painted with such craftsmanship by Luis de Morales.

Because the Marquis's eyes were on her face, she felt the colour come into her cheeks and said quickly:

"I . . . I never realised . . . I never dreamt . . . but . . . I suppose . . ."

"It is extraordinarily like you," the Marquis said quietly. "I have wondered ever since I saw it first when I was a small boy what the Virgin's eyes would look like if she raised them, and now I know!"

The way he spoke made Valeda feel suddenly very shy, and she would have turned away if he had not put out his hand to prevent her.

"No," he said, "stand where you are! I want to see what I never expected to see in my life, the reality of what must have been the dream of Luis de Morales in the sixteenth century."

Valeda blushed again, then she managed to say:

"Y-Your Lordship is . . . very flattering . . . but although there may be a very small resemblance . . . perhaps because the Virgin Mary is fair . . . which is unusual in Spain . . . this picture has an idealised beauty which no . . . human person could . . . emulate."

"That may be your opinion," the Marquis remarked, "but it is not mine."

He looked at her deeply and penetratingly, almost as if he were looking beneath the surface for something he was seeking.

Then his eyes went back again to the portrait on the wall.

He said nothing, and yet in a strange manner Valeda felt as though he were talking to her, telling her how, because he admired this picture so much, it was somehow very important that she should look like it and be for him a dream come true.

He must have read her thoughts, because at last he said:

"You are right, Miss Warde, that is exactly what it is, and few men are fortunate enough to see their dreams materialise."

With that, without saying any more, he turned and walked away, moving down the gallery without looking back.

Because he had behaved so strangely, so utterly unpredictably, Valeda could only stare after him, thinking then what had happened was in itself a dream rather than reality.

While they had been talking, Mirabelle had moved back to look at Bosch's picture *The Hay Wagon* with the strange people playing round it, the wagon pulled by some monsters which symbolised the passions.

Behind the cart came the most powerful men on earth, who possessed all the hay they wanted.

To Mirabelle it was strange and very amusing, and on one triptych were some little green devils which she wanted Valeda to explain to her.

Valeda did her best to make them interesting, and they wandered on through the gallery looking at picture after picture while she tried to find a story about each one of them.

She knew, however, that one part of her mind was still bemused by the Marquis and what he had said to her.

Before they left the Prado she felt impelled to go back once again to Luis de Morales's painting and satisfy herself that she had not been mistaken, nor had the Marquis, in thinking it resembled her.

Now he had pointed it out to her, she could see a definite resemblance, although strangely enough, while she in many ways resembled Hermione, there was nothing of Hermione in the quiet, sweet oval face of the Virgin looking down at her baby with infinite tenderness.

The picture itself was so beautiful that she could only ask:

"Can he really have thought it was like me?"

Yet that was what he had said, and she had known that in some extraordinary manner he had been moved by the resemblance.

He had walked away because he could not express in words what he was feeling.

She had no idea how she knew this about him. He had certainly now made a very different impression upon her from what she had felt yesterday, when she had gone to bed thinking him frightening and overwhelming and feeling sure in her own mind that he would not make Hermione happy.

She could also understand her sister's longing for the position the Marquis could offer her.

She would have been very foolish if she had not realised that the treasures that filled the Marquis's house, like those in the Royal Palace, were unique.

Anyone who owned them would be the envy of the whole world. But would that be enough?

It was a question Valeda could hear her father asking, and she knew the answer quite clearly.

It might be enough for Hermione, but it would not be enough for her!

She could see again the expression in the King's eyes and hear the note in his voice when he had said:

"A very pretty name for a very pretty person."

She had been shocked that anyone of such importance should speak to her in such a manner, and as he did so, she had remembered all too clearly what Hermione had said about him.

About the women he pursued, or, as might be expected, who, because he was a King, pursued him.

"It is wrong, I know it is wrong!" Valeda told herself.

But she knew at the same time that Hermione would sneer at her and tell her that she was only suited to live amongst the turnips and that, in fact, a turnip was what she was herself.

chapter four

THE Marquis, as he walked through the Prado and down the steps to where his horses were waiting, told himself that he was being absurd!

Of course the little Governess from England did not really resemble the picture of the Virgin by de Morales that had captivated him ever since he was a small boy.

Because he was determined that he must have been mistaken in what he had seen and felt, the lines of cynicism from his nose to the edge of his firm lips deepened, and there was a hard look in his eyes as he drove away through the tree-lined streets towards his own house.

Everything he had collected over the years had an originality as well as an artistic value about it.

He was aware, also, that certain things attracted him in a way more alluring than any woman had ever before.

Women had pursued him ever since he had been a youth, and he could not imagine his life without them.

But to him they were dispensable and he knew, if he were honest, that while they played a large part in his life, it depended more on the femininity of which they were symbolic than their attractiveness as individuals.

As he drove along, he was thinking of the women he had known, and realised that if anyone could read his thoughts, they would be shocked at what a large number there had been.

Just like any of his horses which shied at something in the roadway, he shied away from thinking about his disastrous marriage and how unhappy it had made him.

He had taken a wife because it was expected of him. The match had, in fact, been arranged by his father and hers without even consulting him.

But he had accepted it, as he had accepted his title, his social position, and his possessions as an inevitable part of living.

It was only when the marriage vows had been spoken and the ring was on the finger of his bride that he realised he had taken an irretrievable step which made him extremely apprehensive about the future.

In those days he was still young enough to be an idealist. He wanted more than anything else to embellish the name he bore and emulate the deeds of glory with which his ancestors had made their mark in Spanish history.

But after only a few weeks of marriage he found himself fighting furiously against a sharp-tongued and shrewish young woman who he discovered had hated him from the moment she had first seen him.

She like himself had been swept into marriage without realising what it entailed.

Perhaps if they had been older they could have found some common bond in resenting the way in which they had been treated just as puppets in the hands of their parents.

Instead, they had raged at each other every day they were together, making the gulf between them grow wider and deeper.

There had been no question after the first night, when he had tried to do his duty, of the Marquis making love to his wife.

She had been as repulsive to him as if she had been a reptile and, when she had screamed at him to leave her alone, he had been only too willing to comply.

At the same time, they were both aware that they were caught in a trap from which there was no escape.

Because they were of such social importance, there were public duties to perform from the moment they were married.

Wedding-presents were still arriving from distant parts of the country and from France and Italy, where the Marquis's father was a land-owner.

These had to be acknowledged and thanked for, and naturally those who had given a gift expected to be entertained.

It was perhaps the sight of his wife sitting at the end of his Dining-Room table bedecked in the family jewels, which were very impressive, which annoyed the Marquis more than anything else, although he did not understand why.

After a dinner-party at which they had played host and hostess, he often lay wide-awake, tossing in the darkness of his bed, hating his wife and wondering how he could endure spending another day with her in the same house.

It was then, as if it were the only solace left to him, that he would go to the Prado to look at Luis de Morales's picture *Virgin and Child*.

He told himself that was what he wanted, that he should have waited in case he could find a woman like the pictured face which attracted him in a strange way he could not explain.

After he had stood in front of the picture reverently, as if it were a shrine, he would always feel some of his anger evaporate, to be replaced by a serenity which came like a blessing from the picture itself.

Once the honeymoon was over and they returned to the Marquis's house, they had agreed to live in different parts of it and to see as little as possible of each other except on formal occasions.

Although this relieved the tension a little, it was still not easy.

The Marquis's family were expecting an heir and continually remonstrating with him for being so tardy in ensuring that his wife would produce one.

On top of this the Marquis was well aware that his wife, as a final act of defiance against him, was flirting wildly with one of the Royal Courtiers, and he suspected that it was only a question of time before she took him as her lover.

He then became acutely aware that if she did so, he was likely to find himself saddled with a bastard child whom he would be forced to acknowledge as his own.

Finally, to protect the family name, he accused her of infidelity and by so doing, he was to think later, probably drove her into it with the deliberate intention of defying and, she hoped, humiliating him.

When the Marquis was aware she was *enceinte* he thought he would go mad.

He threatened to murder her and she challenged him to do so, saying she would be only too willing to die if she knew that would bring him to the gallows.

They fought and raged at each other in such a furious way that the situation became known, because the servants talked, in the Royal Palace and percolated out from there into the Social Circles of Madrid.

Looking back at his unhappiness, his fury, and his frustration, the Marquis was only surprised at his self-restraint.

To learn that his wife was carrying a child that was not his was a degradation in itself.

To have to meet almost daily the man who had supplanted him, and to know there was nothing he could do about it was a nightmare from which he thought it impossible to awake.

When after yet another furious row in which his wife had jeered at him, mocked him, and flaunted her condition as if it were something of which to be proud, she had left him, saying as she did so that she was going to publish the truth about their situation.

"Let them all know!" she shouted. "What do I care? I am proud—proud and glad to have a child that is not yours, since any child of yours would surely be as vile and unpleasant as you are!"

Her voice rose to a shriek as she shouted:

"I hate you, Carlos! I also despise you because you are not man enough, having married me, to make me love you!"

She paused and drew in her breath before she went on:

"It will give me great pleasure when I have a son

who will inherit your name, your title and your possessions, to know that everybody will be aware he is not
yours, and that you are a stupid, ineffectual husband
who has been cuckolded!"

Her voice seemed to echo and re-echo round the
room in which they were standing.

Then she flounced away from him, saying as she did
so as a last gesture of defiance:

"I am going now to spend the evening with Pedro,
whom I love and who loves me. Think of us together,
and think how we shall be spending as much of your
money as we can get hold of on a child who is not
yours!"

She laughed as she spoke, and her laughter sounded
hollow and at the same time menacing.

She went from the room slamming the door behind
her and leaving the Marquis white and shaking and
knowing he was powerless to do anything about it.

Then she started to walk jauntily down the long marble staircase which led down the magnificent hall where
servants in the Silvala livery were waiting to help her
into the coach which was taking her out to dinner.

In her condition, however, it was easy to lose her
balance. When the satin train of her gown was accidentally caught by the heel of one of her shoes, she staggered, and before she could catch hold of the bannisters
she fell.

She gave a shrill scream which brought the servants
hurrying towards her, but it was too late.

Before they could reach her she had fallen from the
top of the staircase, rolling over and over until she lay
still at the bottom, with her neck broken.

Looking back over the years that had elapsed since

74

his wife's death, the Marquis knew that it was from that moment that he had begun to live as an independent man and not, as he had been before, as the son of an overbearing and dictatorial father.

When the period of mourning was over, his family pleaded with him, begged him, and commanded him to marry again.

But now, as he had never been brave enough to do before, he laughed at them.

"I am breaking with my old life," he said, "and no one, I repeat no one, shall ever dictate to me again!"

Because it was an effort to cast aside the fidelity, the trust, and the obedience which had been so much part of his childhood, he protected himself metaphorically with an armour which he was determined no one should pierce.

He travelled to Paris and discovered the allurement of women.

There were women there for the asking, and women everywhere else in the world. They only deepened his determination never again to be caught and hand-cuffed by marriage.

At the same time, as the years passed he was aware that it would be essential sooner or later for him to have a son.

He had four sisters, but no brothers, and he knew that if he died without a son, the title would go to a distant cousin who had never been liked by his family.

He was not typical of the Silvalas—in fact, in many ways the exact opposite of everything they believed was important to themselves and their blood.

The Marquis also asked himself cynically whether if the family name deteriorated after he was dead, it really mattered. He would not be there to regret it.

Then something proud and very Spanish in him made him want to preserve everything that was fine and noble in his breeding.

As he thought of his mother praying daily and fervently for his happiness, he knew that he could not continue to disappoint her.

"The happiest day of my life was when you were born," she had said to him many times. "I had already given your father three daughters, and I knew what a disappointment it would be to him if you were not a son."

She smiled very tenderly before she added:

"But you were, and I can remember the excitement that seemed to vibrate through the house. When your father came into the room and saw me holding you in my arms, the tears were running down his cheeks because he was so happy."

It was impossible for the Marquis not to feel that he must do now what his mother wanted and make her happy before she died.

She was growing old and was not in good health.

When he had journeyed to England at the invitation of the Prince of Wales to Marlborough House, he told himself that whatever sacrifice it demanded of him, he would have to be married so that he could have a son.

At the same time he did not make any effort to resist the wiles and blandishments of the beautiful women in the Prince's circle, who found him so attractive.

However, a great many Englishmen strangely resented him and were very voluble when they were alone in their Clubs concerning their dislike of "those damned foreigners!"

Then when he saw Hermione, the Marquis thought she was, in fact, the most beautiful woman he had ever met.

Her fair hair, her blue eyes, and the translucence of her white skin were in complete contrast to the mistress with whom he had spent most of his time before he left Spain.

Dark hair with eyes that seemed almost purple in their depths, she had been passionately insatiable, and as fiercely emotional as an untamed tiger.

In contrast, the cool, almost frigid reserve that he found in Hermione was like a drink of cold water to a man who had become over-heated in the midday sun.

He wanted her, he desired her, but found, to his astonishment, that contrary to his usual experience she did not succumb immediately to his wooing, and made it clear that she had no intention of becoming his mistress.

The Marquis had thought at first this was just a pose and continued to pursue her with the expertise of which he was such a master.

It took him a little while to understand that Hermione wanted marriage. Because this was unusual in the women he found attractive, he thought perhaps it was the answer to his own reluctant conviction that he should be married.

He also had no intention of being caught for the second time in his life in a disastrous marriage which would bring him nothing but unhappiness.

He was determined to be extremely cautious and on no account to propose until he was absolutely certain in his own mind that the woman he had chosen for his wife would be right not only socially but for him as a man.

Although he did not expect miracles, he wanted to

find some satisfaction, if not happiness, with the woman who bore his name.

He did not hope for perfection; he was too cynical for that.

But he did consider that if it was essential for him to have an heir and to see the same woman day in and day out, it would be necessary for them to have many interests in common.

He also envisaged that if he were lucky, there might be between them a companionship that could ease the difficulties which he was sure were inevitable.

With a twist of his lips which had become a habit, he told himself that it was more than likely that his wife would fall in love with him.

There had been too many women in his life for him not to be sure of that, and inevitably, although he would be very discreet about it, he would from time to time find amusement elsewhere.

Then again, he would treat his *Marquésa* with propriety and respect, and would make sure that never again would there be a scandal such as had threatened him before.

Nor, if he could help it, would there be any gossip about their private lives.

The more he thought about Hermione, the more he thought she was the type of wife he desired.

He liked the dignified way in which she held herself, which he knew was due to good breeding. Soon after they had met he learnt that the Alcester family tree was one of the oldest in England, and, in fact, the Baronetcy went back to the reign of James I.

He was still, however, being cautious when he invited Hermione to stay in Madrid and meet his family.

When he told them of his intended guest, his mother and his sisters had all, he was well aware, been slightly upset at the idea of his being interested in a foreigner.

They were, however, not certain whether there was anything serious about his intentions towards the Countess of Eltsley.

In addition, he knew that their hostility, although that was perhaps too strong a word for it, was very much placated when just before Hermione arrived they learned from the newspapers, whose social columns were read by everybody in Madrid, that she had just come into a fortune in American dollars.

"I cannot understand," the Dowager *Marquésa* had said to her son, "how the Countess of Eltsley, whom you have invited to stay, should own a huge fortune in a country which is not her own."

"It is not difficult, Mama," the Marquis replied. "Her husband made an immensely profitable investment, which is something I have tried to do ever since Papa died, but not, I must admit reluctantly, with such remarkable success!"

He did not allow his mother or his sister to interfere in financial matters. When his father died, the Marquis had thought it unwise for every penny they possessed to be invested in Spain.

He therefore made it his business to transfer a great deal of the family fortune into other countries.

He had sold the house which his father had inherited in France and bought a larger and more impressive mansion.

He had done the same thing in Rome, and on his last visit to London he had taken the advice of the Prince of Wales's financiers as to what he should buy in England.

Although Hermione had no idea of it, the night before he left he had become the owner of a house and a large acreage of land in Leicestershire.

It struck him that if he did marry an Englishwoman, she would be pleased to know that for some months of the year, at any rate, she would be in her own country, and from a hunting and riding point of view, Leicestershire was ideal.

However, driving back from the Prado, the Marquis was not thinking of Hermione, but of the English girl— for he was sure she was nothing more—who had been standing looking up at the picture that had meant so much in his life.

He was convinced that her eyes, although it seemed to the Marquis incredible, were exactly what Luis de Morales would have painted had the Virgin not been looking down at the Child Jesus.

"How could there be such a likeness?" he asked himself almost angrily.

He quickened the pace of his horses almost as if he were running away from his own thoughts.

As he walked into his house and handed his hat and driving-gloves to a servant, the Major Domo said:

"You will find the Countess, *Sēnor Marqués* in *El Cuarto des Flores*."

There was a twinkle in the Marquis's eyes and a mocking smile on his lips as he walked towards the Flower-Room, knowing that any woman whom he invited to his house inevitably found her way there, aware it was the perfect background for her beauty.

When he had inherited the huge house that should really have been described as a Palace, he had redecorated a great number of rooms.

He often thought the most successful was the one in which he had placed the exquisite pink tapestries depicting lovers, cupids, and flowers.

To combine with them he had added flower pictures of the great masters of the art, and on the ceiling was depicted Aphrodite, the Goddess of Love, surrounded by birds, cupids and flowers, the work of one of the great Italian Masters.

As a crowning refinement, the room opened onto a Conservatory filled with exotic orchids which the Marquis had collected from all over the world.

In the centre of it was a tiny aviary of song-birds.

No woman could be in the *Cuarto des Flores* without being aware that she was emulating the gods overhead and that as a background there were fragrant flowers and the sweet song of the birds.

As footmen opened the door for him and the Marquis walked in, he saw, as he expected, that Hermione was standing just inside the Conservatory.

Her fair hair was silhouetted against the orchids, her face turned upwards as she watched the birds fluttering in their silver cage enveloped by the sunlight that came from the glass roof above them.

She looked so beautiful and her figure in her tight-waisted gown was so exquisite that the Marquis knew, almost as if somebody were prompting him, that this was the moment in which he should say the words she was waiting to hear and ask her to be his wife.

Then as he walked towards her, he knew, although she did not turn, that she was conscious of his presence.

Aware as he was that this was exactly the right setting for a romantic proposal of marriage, he told himself angrily that it was too contrived.

Why should he do exactly what he was expected to do? And was it entirely by his own wish that he was here at this particular moment with Hermione waiting for him?

Then there came into his mind the knowledge that her huge fortune had tipped the scales of his family's approval, until he could almost feel them pushing, propelling, forcing him into saying the words that trembled on his lips.

Moving almost automatically, as if it was foreordained, he came nearer to Hermione.

As he reached her, he realised that she was turning her head slowly and gracefully, looking very elegant but without there being a flicker of surprise in her blue eyes.

It flashed through his mind that it would have been quite easy for her to find out what time he was expected home, and to tell the Major Domo where she would be when he arrived.

She had waited, waited like a spider in a very pretty golden web, for his arrival.

As he looked at her, appreciating the whole artistic effect, he saw, instead, almost as if it stood at the far end of the Conservatory, the picture by de Morales, *Virgin and Child*, looking so very different from Hermione.

At the same time, incredible though it seemed, he suddenly realised that in a certain aspect Hermione was almost identical to the young woman who had stood beside him in the Prado and who was Governess to her child.

"Carlos!"

He was beside Hermione now, and she put out a hand

with its long, thin fingers to lay it on his arm.

"I was told this was where you would be," he said, "and I am longing to tell you that nowhere could there be a more appropriate setting for your beauty."

He knew as he spoke that he had said the words purely automatically, thinking mockingly that it was what any man would have said in the same circumstances.

"Thank you," Hermione said softly, "and nothing could be more lovely than this, and every part of your house. I am entranced by all your treasures, Carlos, and of course—by you!"

The words were spoken very softly, then as her eyes looked for a moment up into his, then away again as if she were shy, he told himself it was all too obvious.

There was nothing spontaneous, nothing left to chance, about the way she was moving, speaking, and looking.

It was just like a cleverly contrived and very experienced act, and he knew in that moment that he would not play the part that was expected of him now, and perhaps never.

"You must let me show you my orchids," he said, moving forward, "and you shall choose one that will not only please you, but perhaps be a little like you."

There was just a faint note of sarcasm in Carlos's voice, but Hermione did not notice it.

"You are so kind," she said softly, "and I would love to have one of your orchids, but you must choose it for me. It is your choice, not mine that matters."

Again the Marquis thought that she might be speaking the lines written by a playwright, which had been rehearsed until she was word-perfect.

He was well aware when a little while later they left *El Cuarto des Flores* that Hermione was disappointed, though she concealed it cleverly.

*   *   *

It was after luncheon, at which a large number of the Marquis's family were present, all of whom he was aware were vying with one another for Hermione's attention, that he had a sudden impulse to see whether what he had seen in Miss Warde and the picture was not just an illusion.

Perhaps, he told himself, because he was instinctively rebelling against proposing marriage, he had been carried away into seeing what was not actually there, and had just imagined a likeness which came only from his imagination.

He left Hermione when the ladies went upstairs to take the traditional *siesta* which every Spaniard enjoys after a large and delicious luncheon.

Then he wandered towards the wing of his house where there was the Nursery together with the School-Room that he had used when he was older.

He thought that was where Miss Warde would be, although perhaps the Spanish nurse might be with her. Then he thought that was very unlikely.

Although he was certain the English girl would not have retired to her own bedroom, it was undoubtedly what the Spanish nurse would consider correct and her right.

He therefore walked along the corridor out of which opened first a Nursery, which was full of toys, most of which were by now discarded as being too young for his niece although there were other nephews and nieces not at the moment in Madrid, who enjoyed them.

Then passing the Night-Nursery and the room he had allotted to a sewing-maid, he came to the School-Room, which was on a corner of the building.

It was a comfortable room, and even as a small boy he had enjoyed the large number of books which filled the shelves on some of the walls of the room.

He had added, when the house became his own, several exceptionally fine pictures that he thought young people should appreciate, and had also replaced the rugs on the wooden floor by a thick carpet which matched the crimson velvet curtains that covered the windows.

He thought as he reached the door that Miss Warde would doubtless be surprised at how well furnished the School-Room was.

It was very different, he knew, from the rooms he had seen in English houses, where, in his opinion, the austerity of the School-Rooms matched the way that the pupils in them were treated by both their parents and their Tutors.

Then, as he put out his hand to open the door, he heard, to his astonishment, Valeda scream.

* * *

After the Marquis had left them in the Prado, Valeda had taken Mirabelle to see a number of other pictures, but the child was not as interested in any of them as by those by Bosch.

All the way, as they drove back to the Marquis's house, she talked about the strange little people and animals he had painted.

Because Valeda knew she must stimulate the child's imagination, she tried to tell her stories about them.

When they got back, there was just time to wash Mirabelle's hands and comb her hair before they sat down to luncheon.

They ate in the Nursery, which was large, and, Valeda thought, well furnished, and it amused her to find that they were waited on by two footmen.

The dishes that succeeded each other were all delicious, well-cooked, and very superior to anything she had dreamed of eating in an English Nursery.

The two children sat side by side, and after they had concentrated on their food for a little while, they talked to each other while Francisca's Nanny, losing her shyness, began to talk animatedly to Valeda.

"I see in the newspapers that your little charge is a great heiress," she said.

"In the newspapers!" Valeda exclaimed in surprise.

The Spanish Nanny laughed.

"We are not so isolated that we are not interested in distinguished guests from other countries," she said, "and your mistress is a friend of the Prince of Wales."

She looked at Valeda with a knowing expression in her eyes and added:

"They talk about His Royal Highness because he is such a success, almost like a Spaniard, with the ladies."

"He has a very beautiful wife," Valeda said a little stiffly.

"Who, I understand, loves him, as our poor Queen loves His Majesty," the Spaniard answered, "and breaks her heart in doing so."

Valeda could not help being curious, but she thought it was a mistake to show it, although she could not help asking:

"Does he make her unhappy?"

"Very, very unhappy," the Spanish Nurse replied. "Everyone in Madrid knows that the Queen Maria Cristina married for reasons of State, but the King was very much in love with the Infanta Mercedes, and she with him. He had never loved anyone as he loved the Infanta."

"If that is true, then it is very sad," Valeda said in a low voice.

"Very sad!" the Spanish girl agreed. "But when His Majesty indulges himself, what can the Queen do? Sometimes she makes scenes, but it does not stop him."

It was impossible for Valeda not to look interested, and the Spaniard went on in a low voice:

"Pretty ladies are always waiting for him. They sometimes force their way into the Palace, but there is no need. He is always ready to go to them."

"Are you sure that what you are saying is true?" Valeda asked, feeling in some way she had to stand up for the King, but not certain how she could do so.

The Spanish Nanny looked over her shoulder as if she thought somebody might be listening, but the servants had left the room and in a low voice she said:

"There is a dancer, very pretty, Eleana Sanz! She has given him two sons and he is very fond of her, but there are others—many, many others."

"I do not believe it!" Valeda exclaimed.

"It is true," the Spaniard affirmed. "Everybody knows. Poor Queen Maria Cristina cries and gets also very angry, but there is nothing she can do."

"Two sons!" Valeda said beneath her breath.

She thought if that was the accepted Spanish way of behaving, somehow she must save Hermione from marrying the Marquis.

It would only make her unhappy, for what woman could tolerate a husband having two sons by another woman, especially when she had produced only two daughters?

As if she knew instinctively that Valeda was condemning the King, the Spaniard said:

"You must not blame him too much. He is a very good King and we are all very proud of him. But he is a Bourbon, and they are all very fine lovers. It is something of which they are extremely proud."

"That may be all right for them," Valeda said, "but I am sure if they are married, that must hurt their wives."

The Spaniard did not reply, but Valeda thought she shrugged her shoulders as if it were of no importance.

'I must talk to Hermione!' Valeda thought frantically. 'I must warn her how miserable she will be if she finds herself in the same position as the poor Queen!'

Then she could not help wondering if Hermione might not find compensation in the fact that she would be the *Marquésa* of Silvala and chatelaine of this treasure-house in which they were staying, besides apparently of a number of others in other parts of Europe.

"It would not be enough for me," she told herself.

She then thought humbly that perhaps Hermione was right, and she herself was so unsophisticated and countrified that she did not understand that those who lived in the Social World were different.

As soon as luncheon was finished, the Spanish Nanny took it as a matter of course that the children should lie down, and intimated that she intended to do the same.

Valeda, however, had no intention of lying on her bed when there were so many things she wanted to see.

She had not missed when she looked into the School-Room the large number of books there were, many of which she realised must have been added since the Marquis had grown up, for they had been published quite recently.

She was surprised, too, that there were novels as well as books by earlier authors such as Voltaire.

Quickly, because a book was as exciting to her as a picture, she went into the School-Room.

As the Marquis had anticipated, she was very impressed by the comfort of it and the fine pictures on the wall.

As she looked round the filled shelves, she thought with a leap of her heart that while she was here she would have time, especially at night after everybody had gone to bed, to read books that did not exist in her father's Library.

She chose two in French and had settled herself comfortably on a velvet-covered seat in the window when the door opened.

Just for a moment it passed through Valeda's mind that it might be the Marquis.

Then, as she looked up expectantly, she saw to her astonishment that it was the King who had entered the room.

Slowly she rose to her feet, dropping one of the books as she did so.

As she curtsied he said:

"I thought I might find you alone at this time in the afternoon, when everybody else was sleeping, and was sure it would be a good opportunity for us to have a little talk together."

"I am greatly honoured, Sire," Valeda replied. "At

the same time . . . I am sure it would seem very strange that . . . Your Majesty should wish to talk to anyone so insignificant as an English Governess."

"You are being very modest about yourself," the King said, "and it is for me to choose whom I should talk to and about what."

There was a look in his eyes that made Valeda feel shy. All that the Spanish Nanny had said to her flashed through her mind.

Although it seemed incredible, she had the uncomfortable idea that the King had sought her out for a very different reason than that they should talk together.

Because she was frightened, she said, without considering that he might think it rude:

"I think, Your Majesty, that I should go to see my charge, little Mirabelle. She is in a strange place and might be needing me."

The King laughed softly, as if he were aware that she was trying to run away.

Putting out his hand to prevent her from leaving, he said:

"She may want you, but so do I! I find you, my little English Governess, very lovely, and I have every intention of telling you so."

He pulled her closer to him, but Valeda, suddenly aware of what he intended, struggled to free herself.

"N-no . . . Your Majesty! Please!" she pleaded.

Now the King had his arms around her, and as she pressed her hands against his chest to prevent herself from being drawn any closer, he said:

"You are adorable! Completely and absolutely adorable. I have every intention, my lovely English flower, of making you mine!"

It was then with a feeling of horror that Valeda knew exactly what he wanted.

As his lips, thick and sensual, were very near to hers, she turned her head frantically from side to side, saying:

"No . . . no . . . you must not! I will not . . . let you!"

"Do you really think you can stop me?" he asked.

It was then that despairingly, she screamed, and struggling frantically in his hold, screamed again.

chapter five

THE Marquis opened the door and stood staring at what he saw, and as he did so the King turned his head and loosened his hold on Valeda.

With a violet effort she struggled free of him and ran towards the Marquis.

While he did not move, nor put his arms around her, he could feel her whole body trembling against his.

Then with an inarticulate little sound she went through the open door, and there was the sound of her footsteps running down the passage.

The King pulled the lapels of his coat into place and said with a laugh in his voice:

"Enchanting! Exactly what an English flower should be like!"

The Marquis walked slowly into the room.

"You came to see me, sir?"

The King looked up at him, his eyes twinkling.

"I hoped you were otherwise engaged, Carlos, and I suspected an Englishwoman would not take a *siesta*."

"You certainly arrived at an inopportune moment, but never mind, there will be other days and other times—there always are."

"She is very young and unsophisticated," the Marquis said slowly.

The King glanced at him, and there was no mistaking the amusement in his eyes.

"Is it possible you are finding fault with me, Carlos?" he enquired. "I have left you the beautiful millionairess. You really cannot complain."

The Marquis moved towards the door.

"I cannot believe, sir," he said, "that there is any necessity for us to stay here in the School-Room when there are far more comfortable rooms downstairs."

He held open the door as he spoke, and as the King walked past him, he said:

"I am going back to the Palace. Come with me, Carlos, there are several things I want to talk over with you."

By the time he had finished speaking, he had reached the end of the passage and was half-way down the main staircase before the Marquis said:

"If you will excuse me, sir, I have a few things to see to. But I will join you later—if possible within an hour."

"Good!" the King said. "I want to hear all about your courtship of the beautiful Countess."

He laughed, and it was a spontaneous sound as he added:

"I cannot help realising that your family's appreciation of her had changed a great deal since they learnt of her surfeit of American dollars."

The Marquis did not reply.

By this time the King had reached the front door, and the carriage was waiting for him outside, drawn by a pair of superlative white horses.

He stepped into it, saying as he did so:

"Do not be too long, Carlos, I shall be waiting for you."

The Marquis inclined his head with a Court bow as the King flung himself back comfortably on the heavily cushioned seat, and the horses drove off.

There was, however, a frown between the Marquis's dark eyes as he walked back into the house.

In the marble hall he hesitated a moment, then moved along a wide corridor which led to the South Wing.

As he went he was thinking he might have expected that the King, who had a *penchant* for a pretty woman, would not have missed the unusual loveliness of the English Governess.

There was nothing surprising about His Majesty coming into the Marquis's house unannounced or visiting some guest he had staying with him without notifying anyone of his intention to do so.

The King treated the Marquis as if he were his brother and made it very clear that, as everything he owned was at his disposal, he expected a *quid pro quo*.

In addition the Marquis knew that on this occasion he was angry with the King as he had never been before.

He had watched him having so many different *affaires de coeur* since the Infanta Mercedes had died, that he had taken it for granted that the King should have first choice of any beautiful women who appeared in the Palace.

He had never grudged him that privilege, nor had

their interests conflicted in any way.

But now for the first time the Marquis thought the King was taking an unfair advantage of his Royal prerogative.

He had certainly made a mistake in thinking that the English girl would be as eager and willing as so many other women had been to accept his advances.

The Marquis walked on until he came to a side-door of the Palace which led into the garden.

This was directly beneath the staircase which led up to the Nurseries. He suspected, although he had no apparent reason to do so, that Valeda had not sought sanctuary in her bedroom after escaping from the King, but had run down the stairs which would lead her into the open air.

He did not know why, but he had the feeling that being upset and agitated, she would seek the solace of the trees and flowers in the garden.

There was, however, no one in sight when he walked across the lawn, which was kept almost exclusively for any children who were staying with him.

It was ornamented with large flower-beds on either side of it which were ablaze with blossom.

Beyond there was a shrubbery which was much enjoyed by the Marquis's nephews who played "Cowboys and Indians" amongst the trees.

He had a presentiment that this was where he would find Valeda.

He walked along a twisting mossy path, sheltered from the sun by the luxuriant foliage of the trees, for quite a long way before he saw her.

She was in a little clearing surrounded by silver-birch trees, where there was a fountain with a stone basin and in it water lilies and goldfish.

Valeda was sitting on the surround of the pool looking down into the water.

Her head was bent and the sunshine turned her fair hair to gold tipped with fire, exactly the same colour as the hair painted by Luis de Morales on the head of the Virgin.

For a moment the Marquis stood watching her, and he realised from the droop of her shoulders that she was depressed and worried.

Then, almost as if he had an urgency to be with her, he walked forward.

He had reached Valeda before she was aware of him, and she looked up, her eyes wide and dark with fear.

Then, as she saw who was there, she rose to her feet to stand looking at the Marquis, and he could see that she was still trembling and her breasts were moving agitatedly beneath the muslin of her gown.

"I am sorry you should be upset," he said in his deep voice after what seemed a long pause.

She turned her eyes away from him as if she were shy, and then as if the words burst from her, she said:

"I . . . I want to leave . . . I want to go home . . . but I do not know how I . . . can do so!"

The Marquis made a gesture with his hand as though he would touch her, then decided it would be a mistake and said very quietly:

"Come and sit down, and let us talk about it."

There was a stone seat under the trees and as he moved towards it, Valeda walked by his side.

They sat down, and she clasped her hands together in her lap as if she were forcing herself to be controlled.

"As I have already said," the Marquis began, "I am

sorry the King frightened you, but you must not take him too seriously."

"H-how . . . could he," Valeda asked in a very small voice, "how could he . . . try to . . . kiss me when he has only . . . seen me once?"

She spoke with a note of bewilderment in her voice which told the Marquis she was absolutely sincere, and he suspected she did not at all understand what the King had intended.

"What happened," he said after a moment, "is the penalty you have to pay for being a beautiful woman."

"But . . . I am not somebody in the Royal circle," Valeda said, "and . . . I . . . never dreamt . . ."

Her voice trailed away as she sat looking helpless, and after a moment, when the Marquis looked at her but did not speak, she said:

"I . . . should never have . . . agreed to come here . . . and now I want to go . . . home."

"That would be running away," the Marquis replied, "and besides, what explanation would you give for leaving so quickly?"

"You mean . . . people might . . . guess?" Valeda asked in horror.

She thought as she spoke how angry her sister would be that she should be involved with the King. She also suddenly realised that she should not be talking to the Marquis in such a familiar way.

Hermione had made it quite clear that she was only a superior servant in his house. As if he could read her thoughts, the Marquis said:

"You are my guest and as my guest I will protect you. But you must be aware that I cannot prevent the King, or any other man, from admiring you or even pursuing you."

Valeda gave a little cry of horror.

"But they must not do so," she said. "It is very wrong, and although I have been . . . told that the King is . . . unfaithful to his wife . . . I do not want to . . . know about it . . . or have anything to do with . . . him."

She gave a little shiver as she remembered how frightened she had been by the strength of his arms and the fact that it was only by a split-second that the Marquis's intervention had prevented the King from fulfilling his intention of kissing her.

Just for a moment the Marquis looked away from her towards the fountain throwing its water iridescent into the sunlit sky. Then he said in a different tone from what he had used before:

"Most women are honoured by the King's attention."

"I think . . . it wrong . . . and wicked!" Valeda exclaimed.

She spoke so violently that the Marquis turned to look at her in surprise.

"Wicked to be lost in admiration for somebody who is as lovely as you?" he enquired.

Now there was a cynical note in his voice that Valeda had heard before and she said hotly:

"Yes, *Sēnor Marqués,* I mean that! I consider it not a compliment but an . . . insult when the King is a . . . married man!"

There was a twist to the Marquis's lips as he said:

"Then you are very different, Miss Warde, from most young women. They would feel honoured by having a Royal suitor."

"I do not expect . . . you to . . . understand," Valeda said in a low voice, "and I know that you think I am very . . . stupid and . . . unsophisticated as H—the Countess does."

She had almost been betrayed into saying Hermione's name, but she corrected herself.

Then as she felt she must make some explanation, she said:

"I know that in England the Prince of Wales sets an example of infidelity, and I was told that your King consoles himself because he is so unhappy at losing the wife he loved . . . but none of this is . . . my business."

She spoke defiantly as she went on:

"I am happy living in the country at home, where there is no one to shock me by their behaviour . . . and I have no wish to . . . know what they . . . do."

There was a lost note in Valeda's voice, which the Marquis did not miss.

Unexpectedly he put his hand over hers, where they lay with her fingers entwined in her lap.

"Now, listen to me," he said, "you have been shocked and upset by something which should never have happened. Trust me to prevent such a thing from occurring again. Try instead to enjoy yourself while you are here in my country."

Valeda started when he touched her, then she sat very still as he spoke.

Now she felt the strength and warmth of his hand over hers and told herself she could trust him.

Although she did not know why, he seemed to be a tower of strength and security in what had suddenly become a tempestuous and frightening world in which she had thought she was drowning.

Then she remembered that the Marquis belonged to Hermione, and her sister would be furious if she knew that they were sitting alone together at this moment and, what was more, she was talking to him as an equal.

Quickly, because she was afraid, she looked up at him to say:

"You are . . . very kind . . . but I think I should go . . . back to the house."

As she spoke, the Marquis saw the thought flash through her mind that the King might still be there, and he said as if she had asked the question:

"His Majesty has gone, and another time I will make sure that as long as you are in my house, he does not take you unawares."

"Are you . . . sure?"

"Quite sure," the Marquis replied, "and when you are in the Palace, make certain that you are not alone."

He felt Valeda's fingers tremble beneath his and said very quietly:

"I have asked you to trust me."

"I do," Valeda replied, "and thank you . . . thank you for . . . saving me."

As she spoke, she rose to her feet and he released her hand and rose too.

"You are very young for this sort of position," he said as he looked down at her. "Is there not some better way by which you could earn a living?"

For a moment Valeda could not understand what he was saying. Then she realised he assumed it was because she was so poor that she was forced to accept employment as a Governess.

"It is . . . not that," she said a little incoherently. "It is only something I am . . . doing temporarily."

"To help the Countess?" the Marquis questioned.

Valeda thought with a little streak of fear that he was being too perceptive and she said quickly:

"I think now I should go . . . back to Lady Mirabelle.

Thank you again, *Señor Marqués,* for your kindness. I am very . . . very grateful."

She dropped him a little curtsy, then without looking at him walked away past the fountain and through the trees towards the house.

The Marquis did not move until she was out of sight and there was just a last glimpse of her golden head.

Then he sat down again upon the stone seat and stared sightlessly at the fountain.

* * *

The rest of the day passed uneventfully, and to Valeda's relief there was no message from the Palace to say that the Spanish Nanny and herself were required to take their charges to see the young Princesses.

Instead, the two little girls played in the Marquis's garden, and the Spanish Nanny chatted away, telling Valeda the gossip of the Palace and of their own house.

Now she became even more certain than she was already that the life these people lived was not for her, and she found herself longing for the quiet of the Manor and her horses.

When she went to bed, she found it rather hurting that Hermione had no wish to see her, and she supposed she was too happy flirting with the Marquis, intent on bringing him to the point of offering her marriage.

"Perhaps she would be happy with him," Valeda told herself. "He is certainly very much nicer and kinder than the King, and perhaps the stories about him are exaggerated or untrue."

This was because the Spanish Nanny had regaled her with tales of the many beautiful women who pursued the Marquis, not only in Spain but in every country he visited.

"*El Señor Marqués* is so handsome and so rich that they run after him like rats after the *'Pied Piper'!*" she laughed. "Very beautiful, very smart, and very be-jewelled rats, but while he plays his pipes he is never interested in them for very long."

The Spanish Nanny laughed again before she added:

"They cry, they beg him not to forget them, but like a Knight in the Fairy Stories which I read to Francisca, he rides away alone."

She laughed again and Valeda felt that the sarcastic note she heard in his voice and the cynical twist of his lips were doubtless due to the fact that he despised women for running after him, when it was he who should be running after them.

It struck her that was what her sister was doing. She wondered if she should warn Hermione that the Marquis was accustomed to being pursued, and if she made her pursuit too obvious, he would soon find it boring.

Then she told herself, knowing her sister despised her for being so countrified, that Hermione would not value her advice. The best thing she could do was to concentrate on enjoying the beauty which Spain had to offer and forget about the people who lived there.

But when she awoke in the morning, she found herself still thinking of the Marquis, of Hermione, and of the King.

Because everything about them frightened her, she had a longing to be home with no more complications to deal with then that one of the horses was off his feed or a slate had come off the roof during the night.

"What are we going to do today?" she asked the Spanish Nanny while they were having breakfast.

"Francisca has a music lesson first thing," the Spanish Nanny answered, "but if, *Señorita*, you wish to go

103

anywhere in the City, you have only to ask for a carriage."

"Where would you like to go, Mirabelle?" Valeda enquired.

"I want to go back and see the little people and the green devils," Mirabelle replied, "and I want you to tell me stories about them."

Valeda was only too delighted to visit the Prado again, so she asked for a carriage and she and Mirabelle set off alone.

Having told the coachman they would be about an hour in the Prado, they climbed the long steps up to the front door, and as soon as they were inside, Mirabelle ran off excitedly to find the pictures by Bosch.

There were several she had not already seen, and she spent a long time in front of *The Garden of Delights* before Valeda could persuade her to look at some of the other pictures in the Gallery.

Mirabelle like the Velasquez of Prince Balthazar Carlos, and thought the small boy on a spirited, if rather stout horse was riding as well as she could ride.

But she soon wished to return to the little green devils and Valeda had a quick glance at the de Morales on the way to them, wondering once again if she really did resemble the gentle, loving face of the Virgin.

They had been in the Prado for only about half-an-hour when a man approached them, saying in Spanish:

"Excuse me, *Sēnorita,* but it is essential that you should return immediately, and a carriage has been sent for you."

"Return? What has happened?" Valeda asked. "What is wrong?"

"Everything will be explained to you, *Sēnorita,* as

104

soon as you get back to the house," the man replied.

He spoke politely, almost servilely, and yet there was something in the darkness of his eyes which made Valeda apprehensive.

She had a sudden fear that something had happened to Hermione, or perhaps her sister was annoyed with her and had no intention of restraining her anger until she returned.

She must have hesitated while she was thinking, because the man who had brought her the message said:

"Please hurry, *Señorita*, it is important."

A dozen questions flashed to Valeda's lips, but she thought it was a mistake to ask them.

Instead, she took Mirabelle by the hand, saying:

"We have to go, dearest, we will come back and see the rest of the pictures another day."

"I want you to tell me another story about the little green devils," Mirabelle insisted.

"I will try to think of one on the way home, but we must go now."

Valeda persuaded Mirabelle, still protesting a little, to follow the man who walked quickly ahead of them down the Gallery. Soon they were descending the steps, and she saw waiting at the bottom of them a closed carriage which was different from the one in which they had arrived.

She noticed vaguely as the man who had fetched them from the Gallery helped them in through the door that the coachman was not wearing the Marquis's livery.

Then, before she could formulate any other impressions, the carriage door was shut, the man jumped up on the box beside the coachman, and the horses drove off.

Only as they moved away was Valeda aware that instead of two horses which had drawn the carriage which had brought them to the Prado, they now had four.

It seemed rather a lot just for driving about the City, and she wondered if the Marquis sometimes used more horses than necessary simply because they needed exercise.

It was a question her father would have been able to answer, and once again Valeda found herself longing for him so that she could talk with him about the strange things that had happened since she came to Spain.

She would have liked, too, to have him explain many of the pictures she had just seen, and, of course, the treasures in the Royal Palace as well as those in the Marquis's house.

"A story, Miss Warde, you promised me a story!" Mirabelle was saying.

With an effort Valeda set her thoughts on one side and started to tell the little girl a long tale about the strange people whom Bosch had depicted in his painting *The Garden of Delights*.

Valeda had been spinning out the story for a long time when she looked out of the window and realised with surprise that they were in a part of the City that did not resemble in any way the tree-lined avenue which led up to the Marquis's house.

It was then that she was aware that the carriage, with its four horses, was travelling very quickly indeed, and she was sure that they must already have covered a much greater distance than that between the Prado and the Marquis's house.

'There is something wrong!' she thought, and wondered how she could ask the men on the box what was happening.

It was, however, impossible to communicate with them, except by opening the window.

As she put out her hand to find the broad leather strap that led down the window of the carriage, she found to her surprise there was none there.

This seemed strange, and she looked first at the window next to her, then at the one on the other side.

It took her a few moments to be aware that the windows were fixed and it was impossible for her to open either of them.

It was then that Valeda began to be really frightened and was sure that something very untowards was happening.

It struck her for the first time that perhaps she should not have obeyed the strange man when he had more or less ordered them to return. She should have questioned him further as to who he was and who had sent him.

However, he had been very firm in his insistence that they should return immediately to the house, which she had taken for granted was the Marquis's. It had never occurred to her for one moment that there was anything odd about it, except to suppose that Hermione wanted her, and Hermione invariably got her own way.

"What is the matter, Miss Warde?" Mirabelle asked. "Why have you stopped telling me the story?"

"I was . . . just wondering where we were going," Valeda replied.

"Tell me what happened to the funny little men in the round ships," Mirabelle insisted.

Automatically Valeda returned to her story, but while she was speaking, her mind was asking a thousand questions as to what was happening to them.

It took her some time to find the answer.

It was only when she realised that they were now outside the City and travelling at a tremendous pace down a straight road, and in the distance there were snow-capped mountains, that she faced the fact that they were being kidnapped.

She told herself she had been very stupid, for the stories in the newspapers of Hermione's and Mirabelle's fortune should have alerted her to the danger of the Spanish criminals who, she had known before she came to Spain, were notorious in Europe.

But while she had been aware that they should take great care of Hermione's jewellery, it had never entered her mind that Mirabelle was vulnerable to kidnappers.

Now Valeda bent forward to look out of the window and wonder where in the wide landscape, which seemed almost devoid of human habitation, they were being taken.

She had an idea they were driving Northwards from the Capital, but she could not really be sure.

All she knew was that the road was rough and dusty, that there was a sparsity of vegetation, and often huge boulders, as if relics of some volcanic eruption, on either side of the road.

There was also a lamentable lack of houses and human beings, and Valeda felt her heart sink as she realised there was nothing she could do.

She had not yet tried the carriage-door, but she was sure that if the windows were fixed, then the carriage-doors would be locked too.

It would have been quite easy for the man who had escorted them out of the Prado to lock the door without her being aware of it after he had handed them in.

But now he was sitting up on the box beside the

coachman, and the four horses drawing them were carrying her and Mirabelle away to some inaccessible spot, where she was sure no one would ever find them unless Hermione was prepared to pay an exorbitant sum of money for the return of her daughter. It was something she would have to do because she really had no choice.

At the same time, Valeda felt herself shiver with fear at the way in which the kidnappers might treat them.

Stories of people who had been kept in caves in the mountains, or in dark, dank cellars in a City before their ransom was produced flashed through her mind.

She also remembered with a shudder a child who had been stolen from its rich parents and killed accidentally while in the kidnappers' hands.

It was only after the ransom had been paid that his unhappy parents learnt the truth.

"What can I do? Oh, God, what can I do?" Valeda asked.

Almost as if he were beside her, she could hear the Marquis say in his deep voice:

"Trust me."

He had been speaking then of something very different, and yet, she thought, only the Marquis might be clever enough to find a solution to this problem.

Then she asked herself a little angrily why she should trust him.

After all, he played a leading part in what she thought of as the immoral and licentious society in which her sister shone.

Their ideas were not hers, and if they had any secret ideals, she doubted if they made any effort to live up to them.

Yet, almost despite herself, she found herself remembering the strength and warmth of the Marquis's hand over hers. Now because he was touching her she had ceased trembling and had become less afraid than she had been when she had run away from the King.

Instinctively, without really meaning to, she found herself calling for him, telling him what a predicament they were in, and asking for his help.

"What is the matter, Miss Warde?" Mirabelle asked. "And why are we out in the country?"

"That is what I am wondering," Valeda replied, "and, Mirabelle, whatever happens, you have to be very brave and sensible and try not to be afraid."

"Why should I be afraid?" Mirabelle asked. "I am with you."

She put her hand into Valeda's as she spoke and said:

"I like being with you, Miss Warde. You tell me lovely, lovely stories, and I would like another one."

"I will try to think of one, dearest," Valeda answered.

At the same time, as she spoke, she thought despairingly that she might have to tell a great number of stories before they were returned to safety and security.

*   *   *

It was nearly two hours later before Valeda realised they were driving up the narrow streets of a village with houses on either side of them.

There were a few people wandering about, and she longed to tap on the window and try to attract their attention with the hope that somebody might be able to help them.

Then, almost before she could formulate the idea, the horses, which still seemed to be fresh after their long drive, had swept through the village and they were climbing higher and still higher up a very steep road.

It was then that Valeda saw a huge building looming ahead of them, and it flashed through her mind, incredible though it seemed, that they were in the village of Escorial, and the building ahead was the Monastery of San Lorenzo El Real del Escorial.

The books she had read about Spain all spoke of the Hieronymic Monastery which had been constructed by Philip II.

He had built not only a home for the monks, but a Royal Pantheon, where all the Spanish sovereigns, beginning with Emperor Charles V, were buried.

Frantically she tried to remember more about it, and recalled reading that while the centre of the huge building was occupied by the Church, there were surrounding buildings which included a Royal Palace.

As she remembered this, she stiffened, and a thought flashed through her mind that she had been kidnapped by the King.

Then she told herself that such an idea was ridiculous, for no King, however promiscuous, would dare to do anything so outrageous as to spirit away the child of a visitor to his Capital and her attendant.

But why were they being taken to Escorial?

As she asked the question, the horses drew nearer, and now the great building high above seemed to tower over them menacingly.

She was aware as the horses stopped that they were not at the main door but at an insignificant one in the side of a vast wall, where there were windows that looked small and somehow lifeless, as if the rooms behind them were not in use.

Then as the man who had escorted them from the Prado got down from the front of the carriage, the door in the building opened to reveal several other men standing there.

These, Valeda saw at a glance, were roughly dressed.

"What is happening? Why are we stopping?" Mirabelle asked.

"I do not know where we are, dearest," Valeda answered, "but we had better wait and see what happens."

"I am thirsty," Mirabelle said, "and I think, too, I am hungry."

Valeda hoped that even if they were to be prisoners, they would be given something to eat.

As she heard the key turn in the carriage door, she knew that although she must not show it, she was very, very frightened.

"Will you please alight, *Señorita?*" the man who had enticed them away from the Prado said.

"I demand to know why we have been brought here!" Valeda said without moving.

"Everything will be explained when you are inside," the man said. "Now, do as I say, unless you wish to be forced into obedience!"

He spoke so sharply that Valeda was sure that if she did not obey, she would be dragged from the carriage.

She therefore stepped out slowly with all the dignity she could muster, and as she took Mirabelle by the hand, she knew the little girl was awed into silence by the vastness of the building towering above them and the look of the men watching them in silence.

The doorway led into a narrow passage, and as their captor walked ahead, Valeda could feel the cold and austerity of the huge stone building.

She had a glimpse of a large square court-yard, but they did not enter it; instead, they started to climb a narrow, insignificant stairway which led to the first floor.

There was no carpet on the steps, and their feet and those of the men following them seemed to echo eerily as they climbed and went on climbing.

Valeda's legs were aching and Mirabelle was pulling at her hand as if she, too, were tired by the time they reached what she was sure was the top of the building.

It was then a door was opened and she found herself in some low-ceilinged small apartments which were, however, very well-furnished.

Yet the floors were dusty, the panes of the windows, which were not very large, needed cleaning, and there was an air of disuse which told Valeda that they were in rooms of the Royal Palace that could not have been inhabited for some months.

Vaguely she remembered she had learnt in one of the books she had read about Escorial that the King and Queen visited the Palace of Escorial in the Summer months only, when the weather was very hot.

Now, as they had come to the end of their journey, she faced the kidnappers and thought that though they were a very unprepossessing lot, they had been extremely clever in bringing her and Mirabelle to such an unlikely place.

No one in Madrid would suspect for one moment that anyone would be daring enough to hide them in the Royal Palace of Escorial, and it was very unlikely that anyone would search for them there.

Then, as their chief captor began to speak, it struck Valeda that perhaps he had some position in the Palace, so that it was easy for him to enter it and to bring in the other men, who appeared to have nothing to say.

"Now, *Señorita,*" the Spaniard who had come to the Prado said aggressively, "you'll have guessed by this time what we require."

He spoke jeeringly, and Valeda lifted her chin.

"I imagine, *Señor,*" she replied, "that you have kidnapped Lady Mirabelle and myself."

"You are quite right," he agreed. "We require you to write a letter asking the young lady's mother to pay a ransom of one million dollars if she wishes to see her daughter returned safely."

"One . . . million . . . dollars?" Valeda gasped. "How can you ask such an . . . enormous sum?"

They were speaking in Spanish so that the other men understood, and now one of them laughed derisively, and pulling a battered newspaper from his pocket, pointed to it and said:

"One million dollars not enough. Ask two or three, Ramón. *La Señora* can afford that."

"We agreed one million," Ramón replied, "and if we ask too much, we may be left with the child on our hands."

There was silence. Then one of the other men said something about Valeda, which she knew was not only unpleasant but lewd.

The others all laughed, and suddenly she was afraid in a different way from before. Impulsively she said to the man called Ramón:

"Show me where I can write the letter. The sooner we are out of this place and away from you criminals the better!"

There was a faint smile on his lips as he replied:

"At least you have spirit, but I expect you'll have to put up with our company for some time."

"That remains to be seen!" Valeda retorted. "Where can I write?"

There was a table at the far end of the room, and she walked across to it, seeing as she did so an ink-pot, a quill pen, and a leather blotter bearing the Royal coat-of-arms.

She sat down and, as if Mirabelle were frightened because she was no longer holding her hand, she stood beside her and put her small arm across Valeda's shoulders.

"What do you want me to say?" Valeda asked in a hard voice.

Ramon made a gesture that was entirely Spanish, and it was obvious he was mocking her.

"Who could express more eloquently than yourself, *Señorita*, the predicament in which you find yourself, and how distressed and perturbed you are for the health and comfort of your pupil."

"That is certainly true," Valeda said, "but before I write this letter, I would like to make it very clear that I do so because I have no alternative. I am appalled that Spaniards, who I thought were a chivalrous people, should behave in such a manner to visitors from another country with whom you are at peace!"

Ramón, who was obviously well-educated, looked amused, but the other three men who had followed them across the room said roughly with an accent which made it hard for Valeda to understand them:

"Come on, let's get on with it. We have to take the letter to Madrid before it gets dark!"

"Yes, of course," Ramón agreed. "You will under-

115

stand, *Señorita*, that my friends are as eager to complete the business as you are to return to the comforts of the Marquis's house."

Because she felt it would be a mistake to bandy words with him any further, Valeda quickly wrote an account of what had happened.

She wondered as she did so if there was anything she could say which would give the Marquis a clue as to where they were.

She had the feeling, however, that Ramón, at any rate, was well-educated enough to understand it, and was also very shrewd about his own safety.

She therefore wrote:

Señor Marqués,

    It is with the deepest regret that I have to inform you that Lady Mirabelle and I have been kidnapped.
    I have been told that for our release the Countess must pay a million dollars, and I imagine you will be informed as to how and where the money must be paid before we can be released.
    I can only say how distressed I am that this should have happened to Lady Mirabelle while in my charge.
    I remain, Señor Marqués,
        Your Humble and Obedient Servant,

        Valeda Warde.

She paused after she had signed her name. Then on an impulse she added the words:

P.S. I know how highly distressed His Majesty
will be when he learns what has happened.

When she had finished writing, Ramón picked up the
note and read it carefully, then he read it aloud to the
other men, who Valeda suspected would be incapable of
reading it themselves.

When he had read the P.S. aloud, he chuckled.

"His Majesty would certainly be surprised if he knew
we were making use of his hospitality!"

The men obviously thought this a great joke, and
Valeda prayed that possibly the Marquis would be astute
enough to think it strange that after what he knew had
happened between her and the King she should mention
him in her letter, and that this might put him on the
scent.

She knew she could not dare to write anything at all
direct or give any clue as to their whereabouts which
might make Ramón suspicious.

As she put the letter into an envelope and addressed
it, she found herself willing with every nerve in her
body that the Marquis would be clever enough to understand.

Then when she had dried the ink on the envelope
Ramon picked it up and threw it to one of the men
standing watching them.

"Off with you, Galiano," he said, "and be careful not
to be apprehended yourself, or we might have to ransom
you for two *pesetas!*"

This brought a roar of laughter from the others, and
when Galiano, grinning, walked out of the room, they
could hear his heavy footsteps clattering down the stone
stairs.

Valeda rose from the chair in which she had been

sitting, and now she said to Ramón:

"Lady Mirabelle and I would like to be left alone, but as she is both hungry and thirsty, I hope you will be charitable enough to provide us with something to eat and drink."

"How could we be anything but chivalrous, as you call it, in the Royal Palace?" Ramón replied. "For the moment, *Señorita*, you will have every comfort, but should the ransom be long in coming, then of course we will have to 'turn the screw' a little. I am sure if your charge is hungry, you could be very eloquent in your appeal for help!"

"I dislike being threatened, *Señor!*" Valeda said.

She tried to speak proudly and with what she hoped was dignity, but when she saw the expression in his dark eyes as he looked at her and she was sure he was in his imagination undressing her, she felt her whole body shrink.

Then as if it were with an effort, he said to the others:

"Come downstairs now, and one of you can bring the *Señoritas* some food and water."

He pushed them, as he spoke, ahead of him through the door, then he turned to look at Valeda again with the same expression in his eyes which had already frightened her.

The door closed, and there was the sound of a heavy key turning in the lock.

chapter six

THE day seemed endless, and Valeda found her voice growing hoarser and hoarser as she kept Mirabelle amused with stories.

She had explored their prison and found it was in fact two rooms which she was sure were the King's private bedroom and Sitting-Room.

The bed was certainly very regal, draped in blue velvet, with the Royal coat-of-arms emblazoned on the headboard.

It was a large, comfortable-looking bed, and beside it was a small divan which had been brought in, she thought, specially to accomodate Mirabelle.

There were no ornaments or objets d'art, and the commodes and tables in both rooms were bare.

Valeda guessed that a regular procedure was carried

out at the end of each Royal visit, when anything portable that might be stolen was put away safely until the King and Queen returned.

The windows looked out over a magnificent view, but as the Escorial was built high on a rock, there was no possible way of escaping without falling thousands of feet into the valley below.

There was also no possibility that anyone waving from the windows could be seen and attract attention.

The doors were of course locked, and Valeda faced the fact that they might be incarcerated here for a long time unless Hermione paid the ransom demand immediately.

She could not believe that her sister would be unwilling to do so, but there was always the possibility that the King or his officials would consider it a mistake to give in too easily to the kidnappers' demands and would prevent her from doing what she wished.

Too late Valeda told herself over and over again that she should not have obeyed Ramón when he had more or less ordered her to come with him from the Prado.

But how could she have guessed for one moment that he was involved in anything so nefarious as kidnapping Mirabelle?

Soon after Ramón and the other men had left them, some food was brought up on a tray. It was cold and unappetising, but by playing games and telling Mirabelle a story, Valeda persuaded the little girl to eat some of it.

As the tray was being taken away by one of the surly looking attendants, she said slowly in Spanish:

"The food was not really suitable for such a young child. If you do not wish her to become ill, I suggest you bring us something better for supper, and also some fruit."

She repeated herself twice to be sure the man understood, but he only grunted, and picking up the tray, locked the door of the room noisily behind him.

Five o'clock came and an hour later Mirabelle was growing fretful as well as being tired.

"I'm hungry, Miss Warde," she complained, "very hungry, and I want to go away from here. I do not like it."

"I agree with you, dearest," Valeda said. "I do not like it either, but unfortunately, these bad men are determined to keep us prisoners to make your Mama give them an enormous sum of money."

Mirabelle had been told this before, but now she was interested as Valeda explained to her exactly what sum was asked and how much it meant in English pounds.

Soon she was again moving about the room restlessly, then went to the window to say:

"If we were birds, we could fly away and those bad men would not be able to catch us."

"I wish that was something we could do," Valeda agreed, "but I am afraid, darling, it is impossible."

"Shall we get out of the window and see if we can climb down the wall?" Mirabelle suggested.

Valeda shook her head and the child began to cry, saying:

"I do not like being here, I want to go home to my pony in England."

Valeda had just put her arms around her when she heard the key turn in the lock and looked up with relief.

She hoped it would be supper and was not disappointed when she saw the same man as before carrying in a tray, but behind him came Ramón.

He was looking, she thought, more sinister than before, and there was an expression in his dark eyes she did not care to interpret.

"I hear," he said, "that the food is not to the liking of the young millionairess. That is, of course, very regrettable, but perhaps by tomorrow she will be back at the house of the *Señor Marqués* with a dozen chefs to cook to her liking."

He was being sarcastic, and Valeda, in an effort not to antagonise him, said quietly:

"Lady Mirabelle is only a little girl. She does not really understand what is happening. It would be kind if you could give her something more palatable to eat. I also asked if she could have some fruit."

"I have done my best," Ramón said, "not for her, but for you."

The man put the tray down on the table and Valeda saw that on it was a tureen of soup together with two covered dishes, and a bowl in which there was a selection of spring fruit.

"Thank you," she said quickly. "Thank you very much. I am most grateful."

"That is what I want to hear," Ramón said, "and you can tell me a little later, when your charge is in bed, just how grateful you are."

There was something in the way he spoke which made Valeda's heart give a throb of fear, and she said quickly:

"When supper is over, I shall be putting Lady Mirabelle to bed, and I intend to go straight to bed myself also. I am very tired after all this unpleasantness, which I do not need to tell you has distressed me very much."

Ramón came a little nearer to her.

"I will console you, *Señorita,*" he said. "There is no reason for us not to enjoy ourselves even if you are in bed."

For a moment Valeda found it impossible to speak. Then she said:

"Go away! You have no right to behave in this ... unpleasant manner, and when our supper is finished, I do not wish to see ... you or anyone else ... again!"

He laughed, and it was a very frightening sound, before he said:

"We will argue about that later. Put the child to bed. I have provided one of the right size for her, and you and I will enjoy ourselves in the same way as His Majesty does when he is here."

Valeda found herself trembling, but with a courage she did not know she possessed she faced the dark-eyed Spaniard defiantly.

"You are not to speak to me in such a manner!" she said angrily. "We may be your prisoners ... but I demand that you treat Lady Mirabelle and myself with ... respect. Now get out of this room while we eat the food you have brought us ... and do not dare to ... come back!"

She thought as she spoke that her voice sounded ferocious and that Ramón would be abashed.

Instead, he just laughed with genuine amusement in his voice and said:

"You have the courage of a tiger-cub, and it will be delightful to tame you! But I will wait until you have enjoyed your supper. Then put the child to bed as I have told you, unless you wish her to be a spectator."

Valeda would have argued with him again, but before

she could storm a response at him, he had left the room smiling, as if in anticipation of the joys he fancied lay ahead.

After the key had turned in the lock, she could hear his footsteps dying away down the stairs.

For a moment she felt she must scream at him not to come back.

Then with a superhuman effort she turned her attention to Mirabelle, who was inspecting the food that had been laid on the table.

Since, of course, Valeda and Ramón had been speaking in Spanish, the little girl had not understood a word of what had been said and was therefore not nervous.

Instead, she sat down at the table, and when Valeda gave her a plate of soup, she ate it with relish.

"This is good, Miss Warde!" she said. "Much, much nicer than that horrid meat we had for luncheon."

Valeda poured out a little soup for herself, but she was so frightened that she felt as if it were impossible to swallow.

She, however, forced herself to encourage Mirabelle not only to finish the soup but to eat quite a considerable amount of a dish of veal and cheese.

It was rather greasy, but because the child was hungry, and it was quite edible, she finished it, then ate some of the fruit.

Slumping back in her chair, Mirabelle complained that she was tired.

"I am sure you are," Valeda agreed, "and it would be sensible if you would go to bed and sleep. I am sure in the morning someone will come to rescue us."

"How can I go to bed when I have no nightgown to wear?" Mirabelle asked as they went from the Sitting-Room into the bedroom.

"You will have to sleep in your chemise," Valeda replied.

Mirabelle, thinking this was a funny thing to do, laughed about it, and without making any more difficulties allowed Valeda to undress her.

Then, looking at the little bed, she said:

"I do not want to sleep in that!"

"I thought we might both sleep in the big bed," Valeda suggested.

"Together?"

"I think we would feel more cosy, side by side."

Mirabelle gave a little whoop of delight.

"I would like that," she said. "I would like it very much, and I would not then feel afraid."

Valeda wished she could say the same thing.

Instead, she heard Mirabelle's prayers, laid her down on one side of the Royal bed, and tucked her in.

"Now go to sleep," she said. "I shall be with you in a few minutes, but I have something I must do first in the other room."

"You will not be long, will you?" Mirabelle asked a little nervously.

At the same time, her eyes were closing and she was obviously very sleepy.

"No, I shall not be long," Valeda promised.

She had already ascertained that the only entrance to the King's room was through the Sitting-Room, and there appeared to be no door from it leading into the passage.

She felt perhaps the reason Ramón had chosen these two rooms as their prison was that the door in the Sitting-Room was a very heavy one. Perhaps it had been deliberately made so for security reasons when the Palace was being built by Philip II.

Now she shut the communicating door between the bedroom and the Sitting-Room and hurried to look at the door through which Ramón must enter when he came back as he had threatened.

There was no bolt, in fact nothing by which she could prevent him from opening the door from the outside.

Then she looked round and started to move the furniture.

On one wall there was a French commode beautifully inlaid with gilt handles and locks.

It was heavy, but somehow she managed by pushing and pulling it to get it in front of the door.

Then there was the table on which they had eaten their supper, and on top of that and the commode she pulled the chairs, which were all of carved wood and upholstered in velvet.

Afterwards she was to wonder how she had had the strength to lift furniture which would have seemed quite heavy to a strong man. But fear gave her power that she would not have had otherwise.

Finally, by the time that dusk had fallen outside, there was a mountain of furniture blocking the doorway, which she was sure would be an effective defence, unless Ramón brought his men upstairs to help him force an entrance.

Then again she was taking no chances, and when she went back into the bedroom to find Mirabelle fast asleep, she started to pile furniture in the same way as she had done in the Sitting-Room against the bedroom door.

By the time she had finished she was exhausted, and it was also very nearly dark.

She noted they had been provided with one small candle, but she was frightened to light it in case when Ramón returned he should be aware that she was awake and might think she was waiting for him.

Instead, she pulled back the curtains as far as they would go, so that when the stars came out, there would be some light in the room. Perhaps also later still, although she was not sure, there would be a moon.

She gave a last look at the furniture stacked in front of the door. Then, feeling sure she had made herself safe, she took off her gown, and without removing her petticoats or her bodice, got into bed beside Mirabelle.

She knew as she did so that she was desperately tired, not only after all the extraordinary events of the day, but also from the sheer physical effort involved in moving furniture that she would never have attempted in other circumstances.

Mirabelle was fast asleep, and as Valeda lay down beside her, she started to pray fervently to her father that they might spend the night unmolested.

Strangely enough, although it would have seemed to her impossible, she must have fallen asleep, for she awoke with a sudden start, and for a moment could not think where she was and what was happening.

Then, as she remembered that she was imprisoned with Mirabelle in Escorial, she saw silhouetted against the light coming from the window a man's figure.

For a moment she could only draw in her breath in sheer terror.

Then, as she opened her mouth to scream, he bent forward, and even as her whole body stiffened at the closeness of him, his lips were on hers, holding her silent and captive.

It was then, as she put up her hands to free herself, she knew, as the pressure of his lips deepened and his arms enclosed her, who was there.

It was not Ramón, as she had feared, but incredibly and unbelievably, it was the Marquis!

He kissed her until he felt her relax and knew that she understood. Then he raised his head and said very softly:

"Do not make a sound! I have come to take you away."

"It . . . is . . . you!"

She could hardly speak the words, and yet somehow they came to her lips.

Then she felt as if there were a flame shooting up from inside her which lit the whole room with an irrepressible wonder.

He was there—there when she wanted him, and she need no longer be afraid.

As if he understood what she was feeling, he bent and gently kissed her again before he said, his lips very near to hers:

"We must move quickly, but do not speak, just follow me."

He raised himself and walked around to the other side of the bed, and by the light of the stars Valeda could see him begin to pick up Mirabelle.

He pulled back the bedclothes to do so, and realising that the child was wearing only a chemise, he took a blanket from the top of the bed and wrapped it around her very gently.

He was, in fact, so gentle that she did not wake, and only when he was lifting her in his arms did Valeda, who was watching him almost as if she were in a dream, realise that he had given her an order to follow him, and she was not doing so.

She slipped out of bed, not daring to put on her gown, but instead, just as the Marquis had taken a blanket from the bed, she pulled off a sheet and draped it over her shoulders.

By this time he was already across the room. As he looked back, she pulled the sheet close around her and followed him as he had told her to do.

Only as she reached him was she aware that he was not standing by the door, which was still blocked by the furniture she had piled against it, but by an opening in the panelling beside the fireplace.

She could see it clearly because, to her surprise, there was a light inside.

She glanced up at the Marquis as if to question him, and he said softly:

"Carry the lantern and go first down the stairs. I do not wish to wake the child."

Valeda, knowing she should not reply, merely nodded her head, bent down, and picked up the lantern, which she found was a small, shuttered one.

Then, as the Marquis had told her, she started to descend a flight of stone steps spiralling downwards.

She realised as she went that it was going to be difficult for the Marquis carrying Mirabelle, because the staircase was very narrow and the little girl was asleep in his arms.

She therefore held the lantern high above her head so that he could see where to place his feet, and she went very slowly, feeling that was what he would wish her to do.

She had not paused to put on her shoes, and in her

stockinged feet, in fact, she found it easier to find each step.

She wondered how the Marquis could follow her so silently, until she realised that he, too, was shoeless.

They continued to descend, and it took a very long time to reach the bottom of the staircase.

Then, as she entered a narrow passage, she could feel the cold evening air and was sure she had reached ground level.

She moved forward a few steps and a second later saw a door slightly ajar in front of her.

Only then did she pause to wait for the Marquis, afraid to go farther in case she did anything wrong.

Reaching her side, he said in a whisper:

"Blow out the lantern, open the door, and follow me."

When Valeda blew out the light, they were in almost total darkness, until she pulled the door open and the Marquis very cautiously moved forward.

He looked to the right, then left, then set off, moving very quickly over paved stones to where in the distance Valeda could see there were some trees.

Encumbered by the lantern she was carrying, and also by the folds of the sheet she had wrapped around her, she found it difficult to keep up with the Marquis, until he had reached the shelter of the trees.

He then moved a little more slowly, and just ahead of them Valeda saw a closed carriage.

With a leap of her heart she knew they were free! The Marquis had saved them and, although it seemed incredible, they were no longer prisoners and had escaped without interference or anyone being aware that they had done so.

The Marquis lifted Mirabelle into the carriage and

put her down on the seat, and as he did so she gave a little cry and woke up.

"Where—am I? What is—happening?" she asked drowsily.

Valeda felt the Marquis help her into the carriage, and even as she sat down beside the child and put her arms around her, he had followed her and closed the door, and the horses were moving off.

"Where—am I?" Mirabelle asked again.

"Y-you are . . . safe . . . dearest," Valeda managed to say, and her voice sounded strange even to herself.

Mirabelle put her head on Valeda's shoulder and cuddled close to her.

"I—am—so tired."

"I know," Valeda answered. "Go to sleep. Everything is all right now."

As she spoke, she turned her head to look at the Marquis and realised she could see him in the faint light coming through the windows.

She could see not only the stars, but she was right in thinking there would be moonlight.

It was not really necessary for her to see him, however, for she could feel him, large and strong beside her, and she had an irresistible impulse to put her head on his shoulder, as Mirabelle had on hers, and fall asleep because she was both safe and happy.

Almost as if he read her thoughts she felt his arm go round her, and without thinking any further, she rested her head against him.

"How . . . did you . . . manage it? How could you have . . . saved us as . . . you did?" she asked.

Her voice seemed to come from a long way away and be unnaturally indistinct.

She felt his arm tighten before he replied:

"It was very clever of you to tell me where you were in the letter you wrote asking for the ransom."

"You . . . understood!"

"It took me a little time," the Marquis admitted. "At first I could not imagine why, feeling as you did about the King, you should mention him particularly, unless there was a special reason for it. Then when I saw the word 'highly,' I knew you were telling me where you were."

"That was clever . . . very clever of . . . you."

"Not really," the Marquis said. "You must realise by this time that I can read your thoughts, and the vibrations between us are different from what you or I could feel with anybody else."

Because they were in semi-darkness and she was so bemused by everything that had happened, Valeda did not argue with him or feel she should refute what he was implying.

She only knew it was like reaching a Heaven of happiness after being in a Hell of fear to know he was there; to feel his arm around her; to know the strength of him and that both she and Mirabelle were safe.

The child was fast asleep again, and was somehow curled up against her like a small kitten. As Valeda looked up at the Marquis, she was acutely aware that his lips were near to hers. When he had kissed her, she had been so overwhelmingly glad that it did not seem in the least wrong but entirely natural.

"How could this have happened?" the Marquis asked. "Thank God, I have been able to get you away without enduring any more anxiety as to where you were or what you might be suffering."

There was a note in his voice that made Valeda know

he really cared, and she replied:

"I suppose it was my fault for trusting the man when he came to the Prado and told me that we must return immediately."

"So that is what happened!" the Marquis exclaimed. "I imagined it must have been something like that."

"It was only when I saw that the carriage was drawn by four horses," Valeda went on, "that I began to think it was strange. Then when we were out of the City and in the country, I knew they were kidnapping Mirabelle!"

The pain in her voice told the Marquis how much she had suffered, and he said quietly:

"Now, thanks to your cleverness in telling me where to find you, you are safe, and I promise you this will never happen again!"

"How was it . . . possible for you to reach me . . . and why was Ramón not aware of the existence of the secret passage?"

She felt, because she could not see his face, that the Marquis smiled.

"I expect you have already guessed," he said, "that you were in the King's apartments, which made it very easy for me."

"Why?"

"Because the Kings who have used those rooms have often wished to be visited secretly."

"Oh . . . !"

The sound Valeda made made it obvious that she understood for the first time.

"The secret stairway is supposed to be known only to the King," the Marquis explained, "but because His Majesty and I have always been such close friends, he had few secrets from me, and I also have been useful to him when he was spending the hot months of the year at Escorial."

There was no need to say more, for Valeda realised that the women whom the King wished to see had been brought to him via the secret passage with the aid of the Marquis, who had shown them the way up the staircase to where their Royal lover would be waiting for them.

She must have stiffened instinctively at her thoughts, for the Marquis said gently:

"Men are men, Valeda, and, as you well know, even Kings are human."

She did not answer, and after a moment he asked:

"Why did you pile all the furniture in front of the door? If I had wished to approach you from the other room, it would have made things very difficult for me."

There was a little pause then as the memory of the terror aroused by Ramón's declaration of his intentions swept over her, and Valeda shuddered and hid her face against the Marquis's shoulder.

He understood, and she felt his anger vibrate from him as he said:

"Curse it! I will see that these devils, whoever they are, are shot for their disgraceful behaviour!"

He was quiet for a short while, then he said in a very different tone:

"There will be plenty of time to talk about it when we are home. For the moment I only want to be thankful that I have been able to find you. I cannot describe how terrified I was that I might be mistaken when I crept up the stairs and found the secret catch in the panelling."

He gave a deep sigh, as if he were reliving it over again as he said:

"It was clever of you to have pulled back the curtains. When I saw two heads close together in the King's bed, I knew I had not only saved the Countess a million dollars, but also found what I had been seeking myself all my life."

The tone of his voice made Valeda look at him in astonishment.

Then, as if she realised that her behaviour was very reprehensible, she would have moved away from him, but found it impossible.

Not only was the Marquis's arm holding her close against him, but also Mirabelle was asleep, her head having moved down to her breast. Valeda could do nothing but try to steel herself against the Marquis's voice, which she felt was hypnotising her.

"I have fought against my feelings for you," he said very quietly, "but from the moment I saw you and realised how miraculously you resembled the picture in the Prado which has always meant so much to me, I knew you were what I had longed for in my heart ever since I can remember, but thought did not exist."

As if what he was saying was like music, Valeda felt her whole heart and mind respond to it, and she found it impossible to reply.

The carriage was moving along swiftly, the moonlight coming in patches through the windows, so that one moment they were in darkness as they passed trees and stone boulders, the next enveloped in a silvery light.

It seemed to Valeda as if she were in a dream that grew more intensely exciting every moment, so that it was not only impossible to think, but hard even to breathe.

Then Mirabelle made a little movement, which reminded her that she was holding Hermione's child and that, if the Marquis belonged to anyone, it was to her sister.

"Please . . . " she said in a very small voice. "You must . . . not say such things to . . . me."

"I want to say them," the Marquis argued. "It is impossible for me not to say them when, looking as you are now, you might have stepped straight from the shrine I erected many years ago for the Virgin painted so exquisitely by de Morales."

He made a little sound that was one of ecstasy as he went on:

"I dreamed of seeing her hair as yours is now."

For the first time since he had woken her Valeda was conscious that she had unpinned her hair before going to bed, knowing it would be more comfortable if it was loose.

Now it fell over the white sheet in which she had enveloped herself, so she could understand that if she felt she was moving in a dream, the Marquis must feel the same.

As if there were no words for him to express himself, she felt his lips touch the top of her head.

After a moment he said in a voice that was deep and a little unsteady:

"What are we going to do about each other, Valeda?"

It was then she came back to reality and knew that whatever they might feel, there was nothing either of them could do about it.

At the back of her mind, although she dare not express it even to herself, was the feeling that if he did suggest anything while believing her to be only the Governess to Mirabelle, his proposition would be the same as that made by the King to the ladies brave enough to climb to his bedroom via the secret stairway.

With a little cry of horror she said quickly:

"P-please . . . we cannot speak of anything now! What is . . . happening does not seem . . . real . . . and today has been . . . horrible . . . a nightmare!"

She was pleading with him, and he replied quietly:

"You know I would not do anything to upset you more than you have been upset already. You are right, Valeda. The questions that confront us can be answered another time. Now let us just be happy that we are together, and I am no longer desperate in case I cannot find you."

Because he had acquiesced so quickly, Valeda put her head against his shoulder, and feeling his lips against her hair, she knew it did not matter.

All she wanted to think about was that Mirabelle and she were safe, and that when Ramón finally broke into the Sitting-Room, then the bedroom, he would find them gone.

Once again the Marquis must have been aware of what she was thinking, for he said very kindly and gently:

"Forget it, it is all over! Never again will I be such a fool as to allow anything so precious, and that includes you as well as Mirabelle, to be unguarded."

Valeda shut her eyes.

There was again that passionate note in his voice, and she knew that the closeness of him was a magnetism that made her feel as if she were flying in the sky.

She remembered the feeling of his lips on hers, and she knew from the moment when she had realised who it was that was touching her, that her whole being had leaped towards him, almost as if she gave herself to him.

They drove on in silence, and Valeda was thinking it was as if she could see the words written in letters of fire: "This is LOVE."

* * *

Later, just before they reached the Marquis's house, she spoke after a long time.

"Please . . . must I see anyone when I arrive . . . looking as I do now?"

He did not reply at once, and she went on quickly:

"Take Mirabelle to her mother and tell them what has happened. I will explain . . . everything in the morning . . . but not . . . tonight."

"I understand, of course I do!" the Marquis replied. "You have been through enough."

As he spoke he took his arm from her and said:

"Go to bed, my darling. Trust me and everything will be as you want it to be."

There was no time for Valeda to thank him, for the horses had come to a standstill. The door was opened and the Marquis's servants stood there in their magnificent livery.

He stepped out, and taking Mirabelle from Valeda's arms lifted her from the carriage as she began to wake up.

Then he said to the footman:

"Take Miss Warde to the side-door, and see that she is helped up to her apartment."

Valeda lay back, the carriage door was shut, and as the horses moved off again, she saw the Marquis carrying Mirabelle in his arms walk up the steps towards the front door.

It flashed through her mind with an agony that was like the sudden stab of a knife that he was walking away from her, out of her life.

This was the inevitable end, and there was no chance of there being any other.

chapter seven

As the train gathered speed and the officials on the platform together with the senior servants from the Marquis's house bowed farewell, Valeda thought she was leaving a world which she still felt was part of her dreams.

She could hardly believe it possible that so much had happened in so little time.

When she had staggered upstairs with the help of one of the servants, who had been hastily summoned to her assistance, she had felt waves of exhaustion sweeping over her.

They were combined with an irrepressible elation because she had been close to the Marquis and listened to the voice that spoke to her in a manner which she knew would always haunt her.

She was, however, too tired to think clearly. After she had reached her bedroom, a maid had come scurrying from another part of the house to tell her that Mirabelle would spend the rest of the night with her mother.

Relief that she had no one to think about except herself swept over Valeda as she undressed and got into bed. As soon as her head touched the pillow, she fell asleep.

She felt as if it were only a few minutes later when she was awoken by a maid speaking agitatedly at her bedside.

Feeling as though she came back through clouds of fog to reality, she opened her eyes to ask:

"What . . . is it . . . ? What . . . is the matter?"

"I am to tell you, *Sēnorita,*" the maid said, "that *La Sēnora* is returning immediately to England!"

For a moment Valeda could not understand what was being said. Then as the words percolated into her mind she sat up abruptly.

"Did you say . . . leaving for England?"

"*Sí, Sēnorita.* The carriages are arriving in an hour's time, but I did not wake you sooner because you looked so tired."

Bewildered, Valeda looked around her and saw that her trunk was already full, and the two maids who had also been packing everything that Mirabelle possessed must have worked very silently, or else she was so deeply unconscious that she had not heard them.

Now she forced herself to hurry and get dressed. There was only time to snatch a cup of coffee from her breakfast-tray before the trunks were being taken downstairs and a footman informed her that the Countess was waiting.

She picked up the travelling-cape which Hermione had given her before they left England, and taking a swift glance in the mirror, she realised that beneath her bonnet her face was very pale. Then she ran down the stairs and along the corridor which led to the main staircase.

Hermione, with Mirabelle beside her, was just coming from the opposite direction, and as she appeared, the child ran towards her to say excitedly:

"What do you think, Miss Warde? I slept with Mama in a very big bed last night, and when I woke, she told me we had escaped from those wicked men."

Valeda bent to kiss Mirabelle, then, as she looked up, her eyes met those of her sister, and she asked:

"We are leaving?"

"Do you think I would stay here and allow this sort of thing to happen again?" Hermione replied sharply. "All the arrangements have been made, and the sooner we are out of Spain, the better I shall be pleased!"

She spoke in a hard, aggressive voice which told Valeda she was upset, and as she followed Hermione and Mirabelle downstairs, she knew it was understandable.

At the same time, she wondered what the Marquis thought about it.

There was no sign of him in the hall, but there were two of his senior male relations staying at the house, who offered Hermione their profuse apologies on behalf of their wives that they could not rise so early to say goodbye.

Hermione accepted what they had to say graciously, then as she obviously had no wish to linger, she hurried down the front steps towards the carriage that was waiting.

Valeda knew that the luggage would go ahead in an-

143

other carriage with Miss Jones and the Courier, and she asked no questions until they had driven away and Mirabelle was no longer waving through the window to those who had seen them off.

Then, because she could contain her curiosity, no longer, Valeda asked:

"The Marquis! Does he know we have left?"

"I imagine not," Hermione replied. "I was told that after he had brought Mirabelle safely back, he collected soldiers from the Palace and returned to Escorial to arrest those who had taken you prisoner."

She drew in her breath before she said harshly:

"How could you have been such a fool, Valeda, as to let them kidnap Mirabelle?"

"I admit it was very stupid of me," Valeda said humbly, "but when the man came to the Prado to say we were needed urgently, I thought it was you sending for me and got into the carriage he had waiting outside."

"You might have guessed that what he said was a trick," Hermione grumbled.

"They were very wicked men, Mama," Mirabelle interposed, "to ask so much money for me, and we are very lucky to have escaped."

"Extremely lucky!" Hermione agreed. "But I am taking no further chances for you or . . . for myself."

There was a little pause before the last words, and Valeda realised that her sister was really frightened that she might be kidnapped, as Mirabelle had been.

When they reached the station, she guessed that from the moment Mirabelle had been brought home by the Marquis, Hermione must have started making arrangements for their departure.

It seemed extraordinary that at such short notice, and

when it was still very early in the morning, the special coach which the Marquis had sent for their arrival at Calais had already been attached to the express train which was leaving for Paris.

Mirabelle was delighted to be back in it again.

She greeted the stewards with enthusiasm and ran round as she had done before, looking at everything while her mother was engaged in giving last-minute instructions to the Marquis's secretary, who had followed them in another carriage.

"Inform the Marquis," Valeda heard her say, "that it is with deep regret that we could not wait to say good-bye to him, but thank him for his hospitality and tell him we look forward to returning it when he next comes to England."

"I will convey your message, My Lady," the secretary replied, who spoke excellent English, "and I know how upset my Master will be that he was not here to make his own farewells."

Hermione gave him a sum of money to be distributed amongst the servants and those who had brought her luggage to the train.

Within a few minutes of their being finally settled, the guard waved his red flag and they were steaming out of the station.

'Is it possible, really possible,' Valeda asked silently, 'that I shall never see the Marquis again?'

Then she told herself that she had to come back to reality and realise that whatever he had said in the excitement of the moment last night, the Marquis was really concerned with her sister and had invited her to stay with him in Spain because he found her so attractive.

And yet, even to think of the kisses he had given her when he had woken her up made a thrill run through her like forked lightning.

She could feel, too, the comfort of his shoulder, the strength of his arms, and the touch of his lips on her hair.

"I love him!" she told herself helplessly, and knew she would love him all her life, even though he would never be aware of it.

Hermione took off her travelling-bonnet and settled herself comfortably in the centre of the coach with a number of newspapers and magazines at her side.

She did not look at them, but just stared out of the window with a frown between her beautiful eyes. Valeda felt guiltily that she was thinking of the Marquis and regretting that she had to leave him.

Tentatively, because she was nervous and it might annoy Hermione, Valeda sat down next to her and said:

"I am sorry this should have happened, dearest, and you must forgive me for being so foolish. But Mirabelle is safe, thanks to the Marquis, and it was very clever of him to save her."

"He should have guessed something like this could happen in the first place!" Hermione replied. "I have always heard there is a lot of lawlessness in Spain, and now, unfortunately, I have personal proof of it."

"I suppose there is some excuse for the men's behaviour," Valeda said, "when there has been so much written about your fortune in the newspapers."

"They may have an excuse for their criminal greed," Hermione replied, "but there is no excuse for the Marquis not realising how vulnerable Mirabelle and I both are."

She paused, and when her sister did not speak, she went on:

"We shall have to be very careful in the future, although I cannot believe anything like that could happen in England."

"Nor can I," Valeda agreed, "but it might be wise to have a guard of some sort in the house."

"I have, of course, thought of that," Hermione said, "and I have already arranged for special police protection when we reach Paris."

Valeda looked at her sister in admiration. She had never thought that Hermione would be a good organiser, but she knew that she must have become one with the importance of the life she had led since leaving home.

She would also have a deeper awareness of what was expected of her now that she was so rich.

Then, because it was difficult to keep her thoughts away from the Marquis, Valeda said a little hesitatingly:

"As you could not . . . say goodbye to your host . . . will he not be very . . . upset when he returns to the house to . . . find you gone?"

Hermione shrugged her shoulders.

"I expect so," she replied, "but that is of no consequence, and although I find him very attractive, it will not matter to me if I never see him again."

Valeda stared at her sister in sheer astonishment.

"Hermione! But I thought you wanted to marry him!"

"If I did, then I was certainly not serious," Hermione said. "Fortunately I was saved from making a complete fool of myself."

"What do you mean . . . I do not understand."

For a moment she thought Hermione was not going to tell her the truth. Then she said almost grudgingly:

"I imagined it would be a good thing for me to be married to somebody as important as the Marquis, and I admit that he is one of the most attractive men I have ever met. But yesterday afternoon, while you and Mirabelle were missing, a letter arrived from England which has changed all my plans for the future."

"How could it . . . what did it say?" Valeda asked in amazement.

"It was from my Solicitors," Hermione replied after a little pause, "and they informed me, as they most lamentably neglected to do in the first place, that my husband made it clear in his Will that if I married again, any money I inherited from him would go to Mirabelle and I should get only one tenth of what he left me as his widow."

Hermione spoke slowly, and there was a bitterness in her voice which told Valeda how much she resented this restriction.

"Oh, Hermione, I am so sorry!" Valeda cried. "But surely the American shares amount to so many millions that you would still be very rich?"

"Not as rich as I am at the moment," Hermione said, "and I have been planning very carefully what I shall do."

She paused before she said:

"I suppose it does not matter my talking frankly about it to you, Valeda, since, of course, as soon as we arrive back in England, you will go home."

"Y-yes . . . of course," Valeda murmured.

"Then I will tell you what I am planning," Hermione said, as if she could not bear to keep her cleverness to herself, but had to boast to somebody.

Valeda was listening intently as Hermione continued:

148

"I lay awake last night thinking about it, and I am going to be very clever, very, very clever! If he were here, it would teach Edward a lesson for trying to get the better of me!"

There was a shrewd, hard look in Hermione's beautiful blue eyes that made Valeda feel uncomfortable, but she only waited until her sister went on:

"For the moment I shall marry no one. I shall accumulate every penny I can to spend every dollar on pictures, jewellery, and other things which will increase in value. I shall also put such money as I can into a private account which will not be known to the Trustees of the Eltsley estate."

She laughed, and it was not a very pleasant sound.

"Edward was always jealous, not because I was so beautiful, but because I was so much younger than he was. He hated growing old, he wanted to be young and virile, and that is why he could not bear to think of my having another husband, and wanted me to be alone."

She drew in her breath before she continued:

"Well, he miscalculated, simply because he did not know that his investment in Texas would turn up trumps. Now I intend to benefit by it, and you can see, Valeda, that when I am rich, so rich that it is possible for me to marry again and not lose by it, I can choose as my husband anyone—perhaps even a Royal Prince!"

Because Hermione was setting her sights so high, Valeda gave a little gasp of astonishment and her sister said:

"Frankly, I would prefer an Englishman, and I have always been told they made the best husbands. I am sure a foreigner would be too dictatorial and certainly, if he were anything like the Marquis or the King, too promiscuous, which I would never allow on *my* money!"

Once again it flashed through Valeda's mind that when her sister talked like that, she no longer looked beautiful, but calculatingly shrewd and, if she were honest, ugly.

"All I want," she said in a low voice, "is that you should be happy, Hermione, and I shall pray that whether you marry or do not marry, you and Mirabelle will be very, very happy."

For a moment the hardness left Hermione's face and her expression was soft and very much more beautiful as she put out her hand and laid it on Valeda's to say:

"Thank you, dear, that is the sort of thing you would say, and of course I want to be happy, although I think you and I have different ideas about happiness."

It struck Valeda that they had shortly before been the same, when happiness for each of them had lain with the Marquis.

Then she told herself that even if Hermione was no longer interested and, as far as she was concerned, he was free, there was not a chance of him being interested in her, except in a way she could not bear to contemplate.

She had left without saying goodbye, and he would remember her only as a senior servant to her sister. Although he might think about her when he went to the Prado to look at the de Morales picture of the Virgin, she would only be equally insubstantial and out of reach.

'I have to forget him,' she thought, and felt as if her whole body were crying out at the agony of it.

* * *

For the rest of the day, as they sped across the countryside, Mirabelle occupied Valeda's attention. When they arrived in Paris very early the next morning, there was a special guard on the carriage which would convey them from one station to the other.

There was also an officer from the *Sûreté*, who searched their carriage before they entered it and assured Hermione that there would be two *gendarmes* to watch over them on the train until they reached Calais.

By the time they had crossed the Channel, even though they had a comfortable cabin in which to do so, Valeda was very tired.

Mirabelle, after being fretful and restless, had fallen asleep, and Hermione was growing more and more silent, even though Valeda was certain her thoughts were on her plans for the future.

It was only when they reached London and Valeda was alone in the bedroom she had occupied the day she had come from the country that she knew that her dream was ended.

There was only an empty future with memories that were too agonising to contemplate.

"I love him . . . I love him!" she sobbed into her pillow.

She cried until only when the dawn was coming up over the grey roofs of London did she fall asleep from sheer exhaustion.

*   *   *

The next day Hermione made it obvious that she expected Valeda to leave as soon as possible.

With a pale face and lines under her eyes Valeda went to see her sister.

Hermione, looking very glamorous in her curtained bed and wearing an elaborate dressing-jacket trimmed with maribu, had already planned exactly what she should do.

"You can take the train which leaves at noon, back to the country," she said. "I have already arranged for a hamper to be provided for you, so you will not need luncheon before you go. I have also told Jones to see that all the gowns for which I have no further use, and there are a great many of them, are packed up for you as a present."

She paused before she said:

"Not that you really deserve one, considering how foolish you were to allow Mirabelle to be kidnapped. But I suppose I should be grateful that you managed to convey to the Marquis where you had been taken and I forgive you."

"Thank you," Valeda said quickly.

"Anyway," Hermione went on, "you will have no more dramas at home at the Manor, and I dare say, if you trouble to take the social magazines or newspapers, you will read about me and what I am doing. There is seldom an edition in which I am not mentioned."

"I hoped," Valeda said when her sister stopped speaking, "that we might see each other . . . occasionally."

"That would be a mistake," Hermione said firmly. "I have never admitted to anybody in London that I have a sister. It would only confuse the issue if I produced one now."

"I . . . I understand," Valeda said.

"I will try to remember," Hermione went on, "to send you some clothes from time to time. After all, you might as well have them as one of those tiresome charities for Deprived Gentlefolk, and you certainly look better-dressed than you were when I first saw you!"

"I . . . I am very . . . grateful," Valeda managed to say.

She did not feel humiliated by her sister's attitude; she just thought it was what she might have expected. Why should Hermione bother with her considering how different their lives were, and how successful her sister had always managed to be?

She went to say goodbye to her niece, but the child was very excited over Hermione's promise that she should have not one, but two ponies to ride as soon as they went to the country, and another pony which would be kept in London.

"Three ponies, all of my own, Miss Warde!" she cried. "And Mama says I can give them special names that I can choose myself. You must help me think of some clever ones."

"I am sure you will find some in your fairy-tale books," Valeda suggested.

Mirabelle was so intent on doing this that she hardly noticed when Valeda said goodbye and left.

Hermione's secretary saw her off at the station and paid for her First Class ticket, although she fancied he considered it would have been more appropriate for her to have a Second Class one.

However, she went home in style and only when she reached the Manor did she find herself noticing how shabby everything looked, although the garden was ablaze with colour.

Spring shrubs of lilac and syringa and forsythia were brilliant against the tulips.

"I am home! I am home!" she told herself over and over again.

But somehow it was difficult not to see the Marquis's

eyes looking into hers and hear his voice saying things which made her heart turn over and over in her breast.

Only the horses seemed to comfort her as they nuzzled against her, and she knew they had missed her as much as she had missed them.

She patted them, feeding them with fresh carrots from the garden, and told the old groom how glad she was to be back.

It was not quite true, but she tried to make her voice sound sincere, and she was sure he believed her.

Only when she went to bed and the house seemed very quiet and still did she pretend that the Marquis was lying beside her, and her head was against his shoulder.

She would feel the strength and the closeness of him and knew he was everything she wanted in life—but he was as out of reach as the moon.

How could Hermione ever understand that it was not his title or his possessions that were attractive, but that everything within herself vibrated towards him?

If he were a crossing-sweeper or a dustman, he would still be the man who was meant for her by God, and nothing else was of any consequence.

"I love him," she said despairingly into the darkness, and awoke with the same words on her lips.

There was a great deal to be done, and as if she had never been away, she picked up her usual tasks automatically.

The Drawing-Room would be dusted rather than have Mrs. Banks, who was getting old, do the job and drop the precious pieces of Dresden china which her mother had always treasured.

There were the horses to be groomed because old Abbey did not do them to her satisfaction.

There were flowers to be picked from the garden and arranged in every room in the house.

Valeda would have felt guilty if she had left the rooms bare, as her mother had never allowed them to be when she was alive.

After a light luncheon, which was exactly like hundreds which Mrs. Banks had cooked before and she had eaten in the past, Valeda went into the Drawing-Room to finish arranging the white lilac in a deep vase, where it had always stood on a small table by the fire-place.

She had changed when she had come in from riding because it was hot, and she had taken a cool bath before she went downstairs for luncheon, and without really thinking about it, she had put on one of the pretty gowns that Hermione had given her.

It was very becoming, but Valeda hardly looked in the mirror before she left her bedroom.

Now she decided she would go riding again a little later in the afternoon and wondered why she had bothered to take off her worn riding-habit.

"There is no one to see me, and no one to care," she said to the lilac as she put it into the vase.

Then she told herself dryly that she would not allow herself to indulge in self-pity, nor would she lower the standards which her mother had set for her, and which she had always kept up in her father's time.

"I must behave as if they were still alive," she told herself, "and wherever they are they will know, and be proud of me."

The vase was finished and the scent of the white lilac was sweet and seductive.

Valeda bent forward and inadvertently touched with

her lips the soft white petals of the blossom.

Once again the thought of the Marquis came to her mind, and she felt a thrill run through her, a thrill that was like a shaft of sunshine searing its way through her breast.

As she longed for him, she heard the door of the Drawing-Room open and somebody came in.

For a moment Valeda did not turn round. She thought it must be Mrs. Banks or one of the servants, and that they intruded on the rapture of her thoughts.

Then, surprised by the silence, since whoever had entered did not speak, she turned her head.

For a moment she felt it could not be true, for filling the room with his masculinity was the Marquis.

It flashed through her mind that she was seeing a dream.

Then, as she stared at him, he smiled, and it was as if the sunshine illuminated the room and a shaft of it ran through her body.

He came slowly towards her, his eyes on her face, moving purposefully, and yet at the same time as if there were no hurry, and he wanted to look at her.

Then she managed to ask:

"W-why are you . . . here? How could you . . . know where to . . . find me?"

He had reached her side and stood looking down at her before he said:

"I think it is for me to ask the questions. How could you have left without saying goodbye? Or without even thanking me for saving you?"

"I . . . I wanted . . . to do so," Valeda replied a little incoherently, "but everything had been arranged . . . and Herm—I mean . . . the Countess wished to return immediately to England."

"Your *sister*," the Marquis emphasised the word, "was quite understandably afraid, but I thought, Valeda, that what you and I felt for each other was different, and you might at least have told me where I could find you."

"But . . . you are here! How . . . d-did you find me?"

The Marquis gave a little twisted smile before he replied:

"It was somewhat difficult to make your sister tell me the truth, but I had a very strong suspicion, when I thought it over, that you were not the Governess you pretended to be, and also you continually stumbled over your sister's name."

He paused before he added:

"It was not hard, when I confronted her with my belief that you were a relation, to make her admit that she had a sister."

"I was . . . sure," Valeda murmured, "that Hermione would . . . never admit . . . that to anyone . . . least of all to . . . you."

"You should have trusted me," the Marquis said, "first, because I always get my own way, and secondly, because I would have found you if you had hidden yourself at the North Pole, or on top of the Himalayas. Had you done so, I would have spent my life searching for you, and eventually I would have found you."

There was a determination in his voice that made Valeda quiver, and after a moment she said:

"W-why . . . did you want to . . . find me?"

He smiled again, and now his eyes were twinkling as he said:

"Surely you have realised by now that I always get what I want, and it is impossible for you to hide from me, even in Escorial or in a small house in the wilds of the English countryside."

She had no words to answer him, and after a moment he went on:

"We have a great deal to say to each other, but first I think you should, as a good hostess, welcome me to your home."

As he spoke, he put out his arms, and though she gave a little gasp, she did not resist as he held her close. Then he put his fingers under her chin and tipped her face up to his.

"I have dreamt of this ever since you left me," he said softly, and his lips were on hers.

He kissed Valeda until the room whirled dizzily around her, and she felt as if he lifted her into the sunshine and they were both burning in the heat of it.

Vaguely, at the back of her mind, she thought she ought to stop him, but his kiss was so perfect, so ecstatic, that she knew it was what she had longed for, cried for, and dreamt of, but had thought would never happen again.

Only after a long time did the Marquis raise his head and ask in a voice that was a little unsteady:

"Now tell me what you feel about me."

"I . . . I love you . . . I love you!" Valeda whispered. "But you know it is something I . . . must not do . . . and you should not have . . . come here."

The Marquis did not answer, he merely gave a little laugh as if to refute everything she had said.

Then he was kissing her again, holding her closer and still closer in his arms until she felt they were no longer two people but one, and she was part of him and nothing could ever divide them.

Only when he once again brought her a rapture that was indescribable did she feel as if she broke under the strain and with an inarticulate murmur hid her face against his neck.

The Marquis kissed her hair.

"How can you make me feel like this?" he asked. "How can it be true that I have found you after all these years? You are even lovelier and more perfect than ever I anticipated any woman, human or angel, could be."

Valeda shut her eyes and told herself what he was saying could not be true, and that even if it were, she must not listen.

"But I have found you!" he said with a note of triumph in his voice. "So all we have to decide now, my precious, is how soon we can be married."

Valeda stiffened.

"M-married?"

She was not certain whether she said the word aloud or it was merely an exclamation in her heart.

Then as she looked up at the Marquis he said very firmly:

"Yes, married" And his eyes were twinkling. "Because I know what you have been thinking, my darling, and because I realise how deeply shocked you were by the King, I will make it very clear that I want you as my wife, and have no intention of allowing you to refuse me."

"But . . . but we cannot! It is . . . impossible . . . I mean . . . how can I possibly be . . . the wife of anyone as . . . important as you?"

"Quite easily," the Marquis said, "and once you get used to the idea, you will not find it very difficult."

It flashed through Valeda's mind that to be married to him would be the most wonderful thing that could possibly happen to her.

Then she remembered the events which had shocked her, and the memory made her shrink instinctively.

The Marquis pulled her closer.

"I agree with you, my precious," he said as if she had spoken. "Spain is not the right place for us at the moment, but I have a number of houses in other parts of the world, where I think we might be very happy."

He looked down at her before he continued:

"I want to show you Rome and Paris, and even in Spain I have an estate in the South which I seldom visit, but where I think we might be very happy because it is on the sea, and our children will adore it!"

He waited to see the blush spread over Valeda's cheeks before he laughed softly.

"Heart of my Heart," he continued, "do you not realise what it will mean to me to see you holding my son in your arms and looking like the picture I have always worshipped? Why should we wait? Let us be married today or tomorrow. There is nothing to prevent us from doing so."

Instinctively Valeda put up her hands to hold him away from her.

"You go . . . too quickly!" she cried. "I have not yet said . . . I will . . . marry you . . . I am not certain it would be . . . right to do so."

"You have told me that you love me," the Marquis replied. "Is anything else of any importance?"

Valeda hid her face against his shoulder before she said a little hesitatingly:

"We . . . we came to Spain because . . . Hermione thought you . . . l-loved her . . . and she wanted to . . . marry you."

"I was aware of that," the Marquis answered, "but

although your sister is one of the most beautiful women I have ever seen in my life, there was something missing, something intangible that I could not understand— until I saw you."

"But . . . you loved . . . her."

He shook his head.

"I thought she might make me a suitable wife, which is a very different thing. What I feel for you is what I never believed was possible for me to feel. I know now it is real love, not just something physical, but also very spiritual and indivisible."

He paused for a moment. Then he said, his voice vibrating with an unmistakable sincerity:

"I worship you, Valeda. At the same time, I want you as a woman, my woman, who will be completely and absolutely mine, and who will never look at any man except me."

"How could you . . . think I would . . . do such a thing?" Valeda asked in all sincerity. "I love you . . . and because my love fills my whole life and there is nothing else but you . . . I am so afraid that if I . . . marry you I might . . . fail you."

The Marquis's arms tightened and he said:

"Because I can read your thoughts, my precious little love, I know you are thinking that you disapprove of the type of life I have led up until now, the intrigues, the affairs of the heart, the lies, and above all, the infidelity of men and women who are married in the sight of God."

He drew in his breath before he went on:

"But all these things happen only when people are not happy, when their marriage is not the perfect union it should be, when they do not have the love in their hearts which I have for you, and which I believe you have for me."

He looked down into Valeda's eyes, which were raised to his with an unmistakable look of adoration, and he said:

"I swear to you on my eternal soul, in which I believe, that I will be loving, faithful, and all that you ask of me, so long as we live."

Because what he said was so overwhelming, and at the same time so beautiful, Valeda made a little sound that came from her heart.

Then, as the tears ran down her cheeks, she would have hidden her face against him.

But he did not allow her to do so, his lips were on hers, holding her captive, making her completely and absolutely his.

Once again he was carrying her into the heat of the sun, and they were burning with the Divine Light of God, which is the real, the genuine love which all men seek in their lives.

Barbara Cartland, the world's most famous romantic novelist, who is also an historian, playwright, lecturer, political speaker and television personality, has now written over 420 books and sold over 390 million books the world over.

She has also had many historical works published and has written four autobiographies as well as the biographies of her mother and that of her brother, Ronald Cartland, who was the first Member of Parliament to be killed in the last war. This book has a preface by Sir Winston Churchill and has just been republished with an introduction by Sir Arthur Bryant.

Love at the Helm, a novel written with the help and inspiration of the late Admiral of the Fleet, the Earl Mountbatten of Burma, is being sold for the Mountbatten Memorial Trust.

Miss Cartland in 1978 sang an Album of Love Songs with the Royal Philharmonic Orchestra.

In 1976 by writing twenty-one books, she broke

the world record and has continued for the following eight years with twenty-four, twenty, twenty-three, twenty-four, twenty-four, twenty-five, twenty-three, and twenty-six. She is in the *Guinness Book of Records* as the best-selling author in the world.

She is unique in that she was one and two in the Dalton List of Best Sellers, and one week had four books in the top twenty.

In private life Barbara Cartland, who is a Dame of the Order of St. John of Jerusalem, Chairman of the St. John Council in Hertfordshire and Deputy President of the St. John Ambulance Brigade, has also fought for better conditions and salaries for Midwives and Nurses.

Barbara Cartland is deeply interested in Vitamin Therapy and is President of the British National Association for Health. Her book *The Magic of Honey* has sold throughout the world and is translated into many languages. Her designs "Decorating with Love" are being sold all over the U.S.A., and the National Home Fashions League named her in 1981, "Woman of Achievement."

In 1984 she received at Kennedy Airport America's Bishop Wright Air Industry Award for her contribution to the development of aviation; in 1931 she and two R.A.F. Officers thought of, and carried, the first aeroplane-towed glider air-mail.

Barbara Cartland's Romances (a book of cartoons) has been published in Great Britain and the U.S.A., as well as a cookery book, *The Romance of Food*, and *Getting Older, Growing Younger*. She has recently written a children's pop-up picture book, entitled *Princess to the Rescue*.

BARBARA CARTLAND

Called after her own
beloved Camfield Place,
each Camfield novel of love
by Barbara Cartland
is a thrilling, never-before published
love story by the greatest romance
writer of all time.

August '86...THE SECRET OF THE MOSQUE
September '86...A DREAM IN SPAIN
October '86...THE LOVE TRAP

More romance from

BARBARA CARTLAND